"Gabriella." His voice was soft but his eyes were ice. "What's it going to be? Do we do this my way—or the hard way?"

He watched her face, saw the play of emotions across it. She was shivering. From the cool of the night or from anger? He didn't give a damn. And if it was all he could do to keep from hauling her into his arms again and kissing her until she sighed his name and trembled not with cold or rage but with need, what did that prove?— except that she was a woman, an incredibly beautiful woman, he'd never stopped wanting? And, dammit, what did *that* have to do with anything?

"For the last time," he said sharply. "Is Daniel mine?"

Perhaps it was exhaustion. Perhaps it was acceptance of the inevitable. Or perhaps, Gabriella thought, perhaps it was hearing her son's name on the lips of the man who had planted his seed deep in her womb thirteen long months ago.

Whatever the reason, she knew it was time to stop fighting.

"Yes," she said wearily. "He is. So what?"

Of all the night's questions, that was the only one that mattered. And Dante knew, in that instant, his world would never be the same again.

The patriarch of a powerful Sicilian dynasty, Cesare Orsini, has fallen ill, and he wants atonement before he dies.

One by one he sends for his sons— he has a mission for each to help him clear his conscience.

His sons are proud and determined, but they will do their duty—the tasks they undertake will change their lives forever! They are…

Darkly handsome—proud and arrogant The perfect Sicilian husbands!

by

Sandra Marton

Raffaele:
Taming His Tempestuous Virgin
November 2009

Dante:
Claiming His Secret Love-Child
December 2009

Sandra Marton

DANTE: CLAIMING HIS SECRET LOVE-CHILD

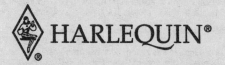

TORONTO • NEW YORK • LONDON
AMSTERDAM • PARIS • SYDNEY • HAMBURG
STOCKHOLM • ATHENS • TOKYO • MILAN • MADRID
PRAGUE • WARSAW • BUDAPEST • AUCKLAND

Recycling programs
for this product may
not exist in your area.

ISBN-13: 978-0-373-12877-8

DANTE: CLAIMING HIS SECRET LOVE-CHILD

First North American Publication 2009.

Copyright © 2009 by Sandra Myles.

All about the author…
Sandra Marton

SANDRA MARTON wrote her first novel while she was still in elementary school. Her doting parents told her she'd be a writer someday and Sandra believed them. In high school and college, she wrote dark poetry nobody but her boyfriend understood, though looking back, she suspects he was just being kind. As a wife and mother, she wrote murky short stories in what little spare time she could manage, but not even her boyfriend-turned-husband could pretend to understand those. Sandra tried her hand at other things, among them teaching and serving on the board of education in her hometown, but the dream of becoming a writer was always in her heart.

At last Sandra realized she wanted to write books about what all women hope to find: love with that one special man, love that's rich with fire and passion, love that lasts forever. She wrote a novel, her very first, and sold it to the Harlequin® Presents line. Since then, she's written more than seventy books, all of them featuring sexy, gorgeous, larger-than-life heroes. A four-time RITA® Award finalist, she has also received eight *Romantic Times BOOKreviews* awards for Best Harlequin Presents of the Year and has been honored with a *Romantic Times BOOKreviews* Career Achievement Award for Series Romance.

Sandra lives with her very own sexy, gorgeous, larger-than-life hero in a sun-filled house on a quiet country lane in the northeastern United States. Sandra loves to hear from her readers. You can contact her through her Web site, www.sandramarton.com, or at P.O. Box 295, Storrs CT 06268.

CHAPTER ONE

Dante Orsini was in the prime of his life.

He was rich, powerful and as ruggedly good-looking as a man could hope to be. He worked hard, played hard, and on those rare nights he went to bed alone, he slept soundly until morning.

But not tonight.

Tonight he was dreaming.

In his dream he walked slowly along a narrow road. It led to a house. He could hardly see it because of the heavy mist that hung over everything, but it was there.

His footsteps slowed.

It was the last place on earth he wanted to be. A house in the suburbs. A station wagon in the driveway. A dog. A cat. Two-point-five kids.

And a wife. One woman, the same woman, forever...

Dante sprang up in bed, gasping for air. A shudder racked his big, leanly muscled body. He slept naked, kept the windows open even now, in early autumn. Still, his skin was slick with sweat.

A dream. That's all it was. A nightmare.

The oysters last night, maybe. Or that brandy right before bedtime. Or...he shuddered again. Or just another resurfacing of that long-ago memory of what had happened when he was just eighteen, stupid and in love.

In what he'd thought was love.

He'd gone steady with Teresa D'Angelo for three months before he'd so much as touched her. When he finally did, one touch led to another and another and another....

Christmas Eve, he'd given her a gold locket.

She'd given him news that almost brought him to his knees.

"I'm pregnant, Dante," she'd whispered tearfully.

He'd been stunned. He was a kid, yeah, but he'd still known enough to use condoms. But he loved her. And she'd wept in his arms and said he'd ruined her life, that he had to marry her.

He would have.

He would have Done The Right Thing.

But fate, luck, whatever you wanted to call it, intervened. His brothers noticed how withdrawn he'd become. They sat him down, saw to it that he had enough beer to loosen him up a little and then Nicolo asked him, point-blank, what was going on.

Dante told them about his girl.

And the three of them, Nicolo and Raffaele and Falco, looked at each other, looked at him and said, was he out of his freaking mind? If he'd used protection, how could she have gotten knocked up?

She had to be lying.

He went after Falco because he'd said it first. When Rafe and Nick repeated it, he went after them, too. Falco grabbed him in an arm lock.

"I love her, dammit," Dante said. "You hear me? I love her and she loves me."

"She loves your money, dude," Nicolo had said, and for the first time in days Dante had laughed.

"What money?"

Falco let go of him. And Rafe pointed out that the girl didn't know he wasn't loaded. That even way back then, all four Orsini brothers had thumbed their noses at their old man's money and power and everything that went with it.

"Ask around," Falco, the oldest of them, said bluntly. "Find out how many other guys she's been with."

Dante lunged for him again. Nick and Rafe held him back.

"Use your head," Nick snapped, "not that divining rod in your pants."

Rafe nodded in agreement. "And tell her you want a paternity test."

"She wouldn't lie to me," Dante protested. "She loves me."

"Tell her you want the damned test," Rafe growled. "Or we'll tell her for you."

He knew Rafe meant it. So, with a dozen apologies, he'd suggested the test.

Teresa's tears had given way to fury. She'd called him every name in the book and he'd never heard from her again. Yeah, she'd broken his heart but she'd also taught him a lesson that still came back to haunt him when he least expected it.

Like that ridiculous dream.

Dante took a couple of deep breaths, sank back against the pillows and folded his arms behind his head.

Marriage? A wife? Kids? No way. After years of trying to decide what to do with his life, of coming close to losing it a couple of times in places no sane man should have been, he'd finally sorted things out. Now he had everything a man could possibly want: this penthouse, with the morning sun pouring through the skylight above his bed. A cherry-red Ferrari. A private jet.

And women.

A wicked grin lit his hard, handsome face.

More women, sometimes, than a guy could handle and all of them beautiful, sexy and not foolish enough to think they could con him into anything more permanent than a relationship—and, God, he hated that word—a relationship of a few months duration.

He was between women right now.

Taking a breather, Falco had said wryly. True. And enjoying every minute of it. Like the blonde at that charity thing last week. He'd gone to what should have been a dull cocktail party. Save the City, Save the World, Save the Squirrels, who knew what? Orsini Brothers Investments had bought four tickets, but only one of the brothers had to show his face.

As Rafe had so elegantly put it, it was Dante's turn in the barrel.

So he'd showered and changed in his private bathroom at the office, taxied to the Waldorf figuring on a few polite handshakes and a glass of not-very-good wine—the wine was never very good at these things even if it cost five thousand bucks to buy a ticket.

And felt someone watching him.

It was the blonde, and she was spectacular. Long legs. Lots of shiny hair. A slow, sexy smile and enough cleavage to get lost in.

He'd made his way through the crowd, introduced himself. A few minutes of conversation and the lady got to the point.

"It's so noisy here," she'd purred and he'd said, yeah, it was and why didn't he take her somewhere quiet, where they could talk?

But what happened in the taxi the doorman hailed had nothing to do with talk. Carin or Carla or whatever her name was had been all over him. By the time they got to her apartment, they were both so hot they'd barely made it through the door....

Dante threw back the blankets, rose from the bed and made his way to the bathroom. He had her cell number but he wouldn't use it tonight. Tonight he had a date with a cute redhead he'd met last week. As for that dream...

Ridiculous.

All that had happened almost fifteen years ago. He knew now he'd never loved the girl who'd claimed he'd made her pregnant, though he did owe her a thank-you for teaching him an important life lesson.

When you took a woman to bed, it was your trousers you left on the floor, not your brain.

Dante tilted his head back, closed his pale-blue eyes, let the water sluice the shampoo from his dark-as-midnight hair.

No woman, no matter how beautiful, was worth any deeper involvement than the kind that took place between the sheets.

Without warning a memory shot into his head. A woman. Eyes the color of rich coffee. Hair so many shades of gold the sun seemed trapped there. A soft, rosy mouth that tasted of honey...

Scowling, he shot out his hand, turned off the water and reached for a towel. What the hell was the matter with him this morning? First the insane dream. Now this.

Gabriella Reyes—amazing how he could remember her name and not the name of a woman he'd been with last night, especially since it was a year since he'd seen Gabriella.

One year and two months. And, yeah, okay, twenty-four days...

Dante snorted.

That was what came of having a thing for numbers, he thought as he dumped the towel on the marble vanity. It made him good at what he did at Orsini's but it also made the damnedest nonsense stick in his head.

He dressed quickly in a beat-up New York University T-shirt, the sleeves long since torn out, and a pair of equally disreputable NYU gym shorts, and went down the circular staircase to the lower level of his penthouse, hurrying past the big, high-ceilinged rooms until he reached his gym. It wasn't an elaborate setup. He had only a Nautilus, some free weights, an old treadmill. He only used the stuff when the weather was bad enough to keep him from running in Central Park, but this morning, despite the sunshine, he knew he needed more than a five-mile run if he was going to sweat a couple of old ghosts out of his system. It was a Saturday; he could afford the extra time.

When he was done, he spent a couple of hours online looking at auction sites that dealt in vintage Ferraris, checking to see if there was anything out there that came close to the 1958 Ferrari 250GT Berlinetta "Tour de France" he'd been searching for. There'd been word one had been coming on the market about a year ago in Gstaad; he'd thought about flying over to check it out, but something—he couldn't recall what—had come up just then...

His hands stilled on the keyboard.

Gabriella Reyes. That was what had come up. He'd met her and everything else had flown straight out of his head.

"Dammit," Dante said tightly. That was twice today he'd thought about the woman, and it made no sense. She was history.

Okay. Enough sitting around. He closed his computer,

changed into another pair of shorts and a T-shirt and went out for a run.

Getting all those endorphins pumping did it. He came home feeling good and felt even better when Rafe phoned to say he'd just put away the French bank deal they'd been after. He'd already called Falco and Nick. How about meeting for a couple of drinks to celebrate at their favorite hangout, The Bar down in Chelsea?

By the time the brothers parted, it was hard to remember the day had started badly, but his good mood evaporated when his mother called. Dante loved her with all his heart and even her usual questions—was he keeping good hours? Was he eating properly? Had he found a nice Italian girl to bring to dinner?—even those things couldn't dim his pleasure at hearing her voice.

The message she delivered from his father did.

"Dante, *mio figlio,* Papa wishes you and Raffaele to come for breakfast tomorrow."

He knew what that meant. His father was in a strange mood lately, talking of age and death as if the grim reaper was knocking at the door. This would be another endless litany about attorneys and accountants and bank vaults…as if his sons would touch a dollar of his after he was gone.

His mother knew how he felt. How all her sons felt. Only she and their sisters, Anna and Isabella, persisted in believing the fiction that the old man was a legitimate businessman instead of the *don* he was.

"Dante?" Sofia's tone lightened. "I will make you that pesto frittata you adore. *Si?*"

Dante rolled his eyes. He despised the sight, the smell, the taste of pesto but how could a man ever say such a thing to his mother without hurting her feelings? Which, he thought grimly, was exactly why Cesare sent these invitations through his wife.

So he sighed and said yes, sure, he'd be there.

"With Raffaele. Eight o'clock. You will call him, *si?*"

That, at least, made him grin. "Absolutely, Mama. I know Rafe will be delighted."

All of which was why Sunday morning, when the rest of Manhattan was undoubtedly still asleep, Dante sauntered into the Orsini town house in what had once been Little Italy but was now an increasingly fashionable part of Greenwich Village.

Rafe had arrived before him.

Sofia had already seated him at the big kitchen table where they'd had so many meals *a famiglia*. The table groaned under the weight of endless platters of food, and Rafe, looking not too bad for a man who'd spent last night partying with Dante, the redhead and a blonde Red had come up with after Dante had called and told her his brother needed something to cheer him up—considering all that, Rafe looked pretty good.

Rafe looked up, met Dante's eyes and grunted something Dante figured was "good morning."

Dante grunted back.

He'd danced the night away with Red, first at a club in the meatpacking district, then in her bed. It had been a long night, a great night, lots of laughter, lots of sex…lots and lots of sex during which his body had done its thing but his head had been elsewhere. He'd awakened in his own bed—he made it a point never to spend the night in a woman's bed—with a headache, a bad attitude and no desire whatsoever for conversation or his old man.

Or for the frittata his mother placed in front of him.

"Mangia," she said.

It was an order, not a suggestion. He shuddered slightly—

food was not supposed to be green—and picked up his fork.

The brothers were on their second cups of espresso when Cesare's capo, Felipe, stepped into the room.

"Your father will see you now."

Dante and Rafe rose to their feet. Felipe shook his head. "No, not together. One at a time. Raffaele, you are first."

Rafe smiled tightly and muttered something about the privileges of popes and kings. Dante grinned and told him to have fun.

When he looked back at his plate, there was another frittata on it.

He ate it, got it down with another cup of coffee, then fended off his mother's offerings. Some cheese? Some biscotti? She had that round wheel of bread he liked, from Celini's.

Dante assured her he was not hungry, surreptitiously checked his watch and grew more and more annoyed. After forty minutes he shoved back his chair and got to his feet.

"Mama, I'm afraid I have things to do. Please tell my father that—"

The capo appeared in the doorway. "Your father will see you now."

"So well trained," Dante said pleasantly. "Just like a nice little lap dog."

His father's second in command said nothing, but the look in his eyes was easy to read. Dante showed his teeth in a grin.

"Same to you, too, pal," he said as he pushed past him to the old man's study.

The room was just the way it had always been. Big. Dark. Furnished in impeccably poor taste with paintings of saints and madonnas and God-only-knew-who on the walls. Heavy drapes were pulled across the French doors and windows that led to the garden.

Cesare, seated in a thronelike chair behind his mahogany desk, gestured for Felipe to leave them.

"And close the door," he said, his voice hoarsened by decades' worth of cigars.

Dante sat in a chair across from his father, long legs extended and crossed at the ankles, arms folded. He had dressed in a long-sleeved navy sweater and faded jeans; on his feet were scuffed, well-worn sneakers. His father had never approved of such clothes—one reason, of course, that Dante did.

"Dante."

"Father."

"Thank you for coming."

"You summoned me. What do you want?"

Cesare sighed, shook his head and folded his perfectly manicured hands on the desk.

"'How are you feeling, Father? What is new in your life, Father? Have you done anything interesting lately?'" His bushy eyebrows rose. "Are you incapable of making polite conversation?"

"I know how you're feeling. Hale and hearty, despite your conviction you're approaching death's door, just as I know whatever might be new in your life is best left unmentioned." Dante smiled coldly. "And if you've done anything interesting lately, perhaps you should entertain the Feds by telling it to them, not to me."

Cesare chuckled. "You have a good sense of humor, my son."

"But not much tolerance for BS so let's get to it. What do you want? Is this another session of 'I am dying and you must know certain things'? Because if it is—"

"It isn't."

"Straight and to the point." Dante nodded. "I'm impressed. As impressed as I can ever be, by the likes of you."

Cesare flushed. "Insults from two sons, all in one morning. It is I who am impressed."

Dante grinned. "I gather your conversation with Rafe was so pleasant he decided to leave through the garden rather than spend an extra minute under your roof."

"Dante. Do you think you might grant me time to speak?"

Well, well. A new approach. No barking. No commands. Instead, a tone that bordered on civility. Not that it changed anything, but Dante was, he had to admit, curious.

"Sure," he said politely, checked his watch then met the old man's eyes. "How's five minutes sound?"

A muscle knotted in Cesare's jaw but he kept silent, opened a desk drawer, took out a manila folder and slid it toward his son.

"You are a successful investor, are you not, *mio figlio?* Take a look and tell me what you think."

Damn, another surprise. That was as close as his father had ever come to giving him a compliment. Clever, too. The old man surely knew he couldn't resist opening the folder after that.

The sheaf of papers inside was thick. The top sheet, labeled *Overview* surprised him.

"This is about a ranch," he said, glancing up.

"Not just a ranch, Dante. It is about Viera y Filho. Viera and Son. The name of an enormous *fazenda* in Brazil."

Dante's eyes narrowed. "Brazil?"

"*Sì.*" His father's mouth twitched. "You have heard of the place, I assume?"

"Very amusing."

"The ranch covers tens of thousands of acres."

"And?"

"And," Cesare said with a casual shrug, "I wish to purchase it."

Dante stared at his father. Cesare owned a sanitation company. A construction company. Real estate. But a ranch?

"What the hell for?"

"It is, according to those documents, a good investment."

"So is the Empire State Building."

"I know the owner," Cesare said, ignoring the remark. "Juan Viera. Well, I did, years ago. We, ah, we had some business dealings together."

Dante laughed. "I'll bet."

"He came to me for a loan. I turned him down."

"So?"

"So, he is ill. And I feel guilty. I should have—" Cesare's eyes went flat. "You find this amusing?"

"You? Feeling guilt? Come on, Father. This is me, not Isabella or Anna. You don't know the meaning of the word."

"Viera is dying. His only son, Arturo, will inherit the property. The boy is unfit. The ranch has been in the Viera family for two centuries, but Arturo will lose it, one way or another, before Viera is cold in the ground."

"Let me get this straight. You expect me to believe your motives are purely altruistic? That you want to buy this ranch to save it?"

"I know you do not think highly of me—"

Dante laughed.

"Perhaps I have done some things I regret. Don't look so shocked, *mio figlio*. A man nearing the end of his life is entitled to begin thinking about the disposition of his immortal soul."

Dante put the folder on the desk. This was turning into one hell of a strange day.

"I ask only that you fly to Brazil, look things over and, if you deem it appropriate, make an offer on the ranch."

"The market's going to hell in a hand basket and you expect me to set aside my work, fly to South America and make an enemy of yours an offer he cannot refuse?"

"Very amusing. And very incorrect. Viera is not my enemy."

"Whatever. The point is, I am busy. I have no time to stomp around in cow manure just so you can assuage a guilty conscience."

"This is a far simpler thing than I asked of your brother."

"Yeah, well, whatever you asked him, I'll bet he told you what I'm going to tell you." Dante shot to his feet. "You can take your so-called conscience and—"

"Have you ever been to Brazil, Dante? Do you know anything about it?"

Dante's jaw tightened. The only thing he knew about Brazil was that it was Gabriella Reyes's birthplace, and what the hell did she have to do with anything?

"I've been to Sao Paulo," he said coldly. "On business."

"Business. For that company of yours."

"It's called Orsini Investments," Dante said, even more coldly.

"It is said you are excellent at negotiating."

"So?"

His father shrugged. "Why ask a stranger for help when one's own son is considered the best?"

A compliment? Pure bull, sure, but, dammit, it hit its mark. Why not admit that?

"Well," Cesare said, on a dramatic sigh, "if you will not do this thing…"

Dante looked at his father. "I can only spare a couple of days."

His father smiled. "That will surely be enough. And, who knows? You might even learn something new."

"About?"

Cesare smiled again. "About negotiating, *mio figlio*. About negotiating."

A world away, more than five thousand miles southwest of New York, Gabriella Reyes sat on the veranda of the big house in which she'd grown up.

Back then the house, the veranda, the *fazenda* itself had been magnificent.

Not anymore. Everything was different now.

So was she.

As a child on this ranch, she'd been scrawny, all legs and pigtails. Shy to the point of being tongue-tied. Her father had hated that about her; the truth was, she couldn't think of anything about herself that he hadn't hated.

This place, the verandah, had been her sanctuary. Hers and her brother's. Arturo had been even less favored by their father than she had been.

Arturo had left the ranch the day he turned eighteen. She had missed him terribly but she'd understood, he'd had to leave this place to survive.

At eighteen, Gabriella had suddenly blossomed. The ugly ducking had become a swan. She hadn't seen it but others did, including a North American who had seen her on a street in Bonito, doubled back and handed her his business card. A week later she'd flown to New York and landed her first modeling assignment. She'd loved her work…

And she'd met a man.

She'd been happy, at least for a little while.

Now, she was back at Viera y Filho. Her father was dead. So was her brother. The man was gone from her life. She was alone in this sad, silent house, but then, one way or another, she had always been alone.

Even when she had been Dante Orsini's lover.

Perhaps never as much as when she had been Dante's lover, if she had ever really been that. She had warmed his bed but not his heart, and why was she wasting time thinking of him? There was no point in it, no reason, no logic—

"Senhorita?"

Gabriella looked up into the worried face of the *ama* who had all but raised her. *"Sim, Yara?"*

"Ele chama lhe."

Gabriella shot to her feet and hurried into the house. He was calling for her! How could she have forgotten, even for a moment?

She was not alone. Not anymore.

CHAPTER TWO

HE FLEW to Brazil by commercial jet. Falco was using the Orsini plane.

Based on the way they were dressed, he figured that most of the other passengers in the first-class cabin were going to Campo Grande on vacation. The city was near something called the Pantanal. His travel agent had started gushing about the area's trails, the canoeing, the amazing variety of wildlife.

Dante had cut her short.

"Just book me into a decent hotel and arrange for a rental car," he'd said curtly.

He was most assuredly not heading to South America for pleasure.

This was strictly business. His father's business, and that he'd let Cesare push the right buttons ticked him off no end.

"Mr. Orsini," the flight attendant said pleasantly, "may I get you something?"

Somebody to examine my head, Dante thought grimly.

"Sir? Something to drink?"

He asked for red wine; she launched into a listing of the choices available and he stopped himself from snarling at her the way he'd snarled at the travel agent.

"Your choice," he said, before she could ask him anything else.

Then he opened his briefcase and read through the papers his father had given him.

They didn't tell him very much that he didn't already know. The Viera ranch ran thousands of head of cattle as well as a relatively small number of horses. It had been owned by the same family for generations.

A vellum business card bore the name, phone number and address of Juan Viera's lawyer. A note in Cesare's handwriting was scrawled on the back:

"Deal through him, not through the Vieras."

Fine.

He'd call the man first thing, maybe even tonight. Brazilians kept late hours; the times he'd been in Sao Paulo on business, dinner never started much before 10 p.m. Whenever he called the lawyer, he would request an immediate meeting. He'd explain the purpose of his visit and make an offer for the ranch.

How long could that take? Maybe not even the two days he'd allocated for it.

He felt his mood lighten. With luck, he might be heading back to New York in no time.

It was midevening when he stepped off the plane.

Thanks to the time change, he'd lost two hours. Too late to phone Viera's attorney and maybe that was just as well. All he wanted to do after the seemingly endless flight was pick up a car, get to his hotel, shower and eat something prepared by a human being instead of an airline catering service's assembly line.

The hotel, in the town of Bonito, maybe twenty minutes from the Campo Grande Airport, met the requirements he'd laid out to his travel agent. It was comfortable and quiet, as was his suite. He showered, changed into a pale blue cotton shirt and faded jeans. Room service sent up a rare steak, green salad and a pot of coffee, and Dante settled down to leaf through the documents again.

Maybe he'd missed something the first time.

Ten minutes later he tossed the papers aside. No. He hadn't missed anything. What he'd hoped to see was something about the *filho* of Viera y Filho. Why Cesare was so convinced that the son's stewardship would lead to disaster. A hint as to why his father should give a damn.

But there was nothing.

Dante took a bottle of beer from the minibar, opened it and stepped onto a small balcony that overlooked a moonlit pool. He was exhausted but he knew he wouldn't sleep. The long flight, the time change, the fact that he was still angry at being here…

If a man carved time out of a busy week to fly more than 5,000 miles, it should be for a better reason than running an errand he didn't understand for a father he didn't respect.

Like conducting business for Orsini Brothers. Or kicking back and enjoying a vacation.

Or locating Gabriella.

Dante scowled, lifted the bottle of beer and took a long swallow.

Where had that come from? Why would he want to locate her? For starters, Brazil was an enormous country. He had no idea what part she was from, no certainty she'd returned there. Rafe's girlfriend, Miss Germany 2000-something-or-other, Rafe's *former* girlfriend, a model the same as Gabriella, had once said that was what she'd heard.

Not that he'd asked, Dante thought quickly.

He'd just sort of wondered, out loud, if Rafe's ex had known her.

Dammit, why was he even thinking about Gabriella? The affair had been fun while it lasted. A couple of months, that was all, and then she'd slipped out of his life or maybe he'd slipped out of hers….

Okay. So it hadn't been quite like that.

He'd gone away on business, a trip Nick was supposed to make but Nick had had other things going on and Dante had offered to go in his place.

"You sure?" Nick had said. "Because I can just postpone this for a week…"

"No," Dante had said, "no, that's fine. I can use a break in routine."

So he'd flown to Rome or maybe it was Paris, and he hadn't said anything about leaving to Gabriella because why would he? They were dating, that was all. Dating exclusively because that was how he did things, one woman at a time while it lasted, but dating was all it was.

While he was away it had hit him that the thing with Gabriella had pretty much run its course. He'd gone to Tiffany's as soon as he got back, bought a pair of diamond earrings, phoned her, arranged to meet her at Perse for dinner.

He'd been uncommonly nervous through the meal. Ridiculous, when he'd been through moments like this many times before. Finally, over coffee, he'd taken her hand.

"Gabriella. I have something to tell you."

"And I…I have something to tell you, too."

Her voice had been a whisper. Her cheeks had been flushed. Hell. She was going to tell him she'd fallen in love with him. He'd lived this scene before; he knew the warning signs. So he'd moved fast, put the little box that held the earrings on the table between them and said, quickly, how fond he was of her but how busy things had suddenly become at work, how he wished her the best of luck and if she ever needed him for anything…

She hadn't said a word.

The flush had left her cheeks. In fact, she'd gone white. Then she'd pushed back her chair and walked out of the restaurant, leaving the earrings, leaving him, just walked, head up, spine straight, never once looked back.

Dante tossed back the last of the beer, exchanged his jeans for shorts and went out for a run. When he returned an hour later, he tumbled into bed and slept, dream free, until the wake-up call from the front desk awakened him the next morning.

Eduardo de Souza, the Viera attorney, sounded pleasant enough.

Dante explained he was the son of an old acquaintance of Juan Viera and asked if they could meet as soon as possible.

"Ah," de Souza said, on a long sigh. "And your father knows what has happened?"

That Viera was dying? That the man's son was about to inherit the Viera ranch?

"Yes," Dante said, "he does. That's why I'm here, *senhor.*" He paused, unsure of how the lawyer would react. "My father wishes to buy the place from him."

Silence. Then de Souza, sounding puzzled, said, "From whom?"

"From Viera. From the estate. Look, *senhor,* if we could meet to discuss this…"

"Indeed. I can see we have much to discuss…but little time in which to do it. I am, in fact, on my way to the Viera *fazenda* right now. Can you meet me there?"

De Souza gave him directions, told him to watch for a turnoff about thirty miles from town.

"The sign is gone, I am afraid, but you will know you are in the right place because it will be the only turnoff for miles in any direction. Just drive through the gate. It is perhaps one mile from there to the house."

Dante found the turnoff without any difficulty. The gate was open, the gravel road ahead pockmarked with holes. After about a mile, a house and half a dozen outbuildings came into view. A corral stood off to one side of the clearing.

Dante frowned. The buildings, including the house, gave off a general sense of neglect. The corral enclosed only weeds. There were some vehicles in the clearing: a few well-used pickups, cars with mud caked on their wheels, and an enormous SUV, all gleaming black paint and shiny chrome. Stupid to dislike a vehicle, Dante knew, but he disliked this thing on sight.

Slowly he stepped from his car. This was a successful ranch? Maybe he'd taken the wrong road…

"*Senhor* Orsini?"

A short, stout man was hurrying down the steps, patting his sweating face with a handkerchief.

"*Senhor* de Souza?" Dante extended his hand. "It's good to meet you, sir."

"I tried to delay things, *senhor,* but there was some impatience. You understand."

Delay what? Dante started to ask, but the lawyer clutched his elbow and hurried him into the house. Men stood in little clusters, arms folded. One man, huge in girth and height, dressed like a movie villain in black and puffing on a cigar that filled the room with its stink, stood alone. Dante pegged him instantly as the owner of the SUV. A wide staircase rose toward the second floor; in front of it stood a guy in a shiny suit, rattling away in indecipherable

Brazilian Portuguese. Every now and then, one of the spectators grunted in response.

Dante frowned. "What's going on here?"

"Why, the auction, of course," de Souza whispered. "Of the ranch. By the bank." An expressive shrug. "You know."

No, Dante thought furiously, he did not know. His father had sent him into a situation without giving him any of the necessary facts. He grabbed the lawyer's arm, dragged him into a corner.

"Juan Viera is selling the place?"

The little man's eyebrows lifted. "Juan Viera is dead, *senhor.*"

Dead? Dante took a breath. "His son, then? Arturo is selling it?"

"Arturo is dead, too. Is that not why you are here? To bid on Viera y Filho?"

"Well, yeah, but I had no idea that—"

"You must be prepared to bid strongly, *senhor.*"

Hell. This was not a way to do business.

"What's the place worth?"

The lawyer quoted a figure in Brazilian *reals,* quickly amended it to its U.S. dollar equivalent.

"That's it? Fifty thousand is all?"

"That will cover the money owed the bank." De Souza hesitated. "But if *you* bid, you will have to go much higher." His voice fell to a whisper. "There is another interested party, you see."

Dante had been to auctions before. He'd bought a couple of paintings at Sotheby's. There was often another interested party but Sotheby's hadn't been like this. There was a sense of something not just competitive but raw in the air.

"Okay. What's the bid up to?"

The lawyer listened. "Twenty thousand *reals*. Half what the bank wants."

Dante nodded. This wasn't his money, it was his old man's. Spend what you must, Cesare had ended up telling him, up to half a million bucks. That gave him significant leeway—and the sooner this was over, the sooner he could leave.

"Bid one hundred thousand."

The lawyer cleared his throat. Called out the amount in *reals*. The room fell silent. Everyone looked first at Dante, then at the big guy in black who slowly turned and looked at him, too. Dante held the man's gaze until he shifted the cigar from one side of his mouth to the other and showed all his teeth in what no one in his right mind would ever call a smile.

"Two hundred thousand dollars, U.S.," the man said, in lightly accented English.

There were audible gasps from the others.

What was this? A contest over what looked like a place that would suck in tens, maybe hundreds of thousands to put right? Maybe Cesare was nuts, Dante thought, but he wasn't, and hadn't his father said he was handing this off to him because of his business expertise?

Dante shrugged. "You want it that bad," he started to say…

And then a voice as soft as the petal of a rose said his name and he knew, God, he knew who it was even before he turned to the stairs and saw her.

Gabriella's heart was pounding.

It was Dante. But it couldn't be. He was a bitter memory from another time, another place…

"Gabriella?"

Deus, he was real!

Almost a year and a half had gone by and yet everything about him was familiar. His broad shoulders and long, leanly muscled body. The hard planes and angles of his face. His eyes, the palest shade of blue.

And his mouth. Firm and sensual, and even now she remembered the feel of it against hers.

He was moving toward her. She shook her head, stepped back. She knew she could not let him touch her. If he did, she might crumple. All the nights she'd thought of him. Willed herself *not* to think of him. Told herself she hated him, that she hoped and prayed she would never see him again...

True, all of it.

And yet, standing in the shadows of the second-floor landing, listening as her fate was decided by a group of faceless men, she'd heard his voice and reacted with the predictability of Pavlov's dog, her heart racing, her lips readying to curve in a smile.

She drew a deep, unsteady breath.

Those days were gone. She had no reason to smile at this man. She felt nothing for him. Not even hatred. The sight of him had stunned her, that was all...

Unless...unless he had come for her. In the darkest hours of the darkest nights, even despising him, she had wept for him. For his touch. And sometimes...sometimes, she had dared to dream that he had discovered her secret, that he was coming to her, coming for her...

"What are you doing here?" he said.

His bewildered question shattered the last of those ridiculous dreams. Reality rushed in and with it, the cold knowledge that she had to get rid of him as quickly as possible. Her heart was racing again, this time with trepidation, but the recent changes in her life had brought back the ingrained habits of childhood, and she drew herself up and met his confusion with calm resolution.

"I think a far better question is, what are *you* doing here?"

He looked surprised. Well, why wouldn't he? He was a man who never had to answer to anyone.

"I'm here on business."

"What kind of business would bring you to the end of the earth?"

"I came to buy this ranch."

She felt the color leave her face.

"Viera y Filho," he said impatiently, "and you still haven't answered *my* question."

A sigh swept through the room, followed by the sound of a man's unpleasant laughter. She saw Dante turn toward Andre Ferrantes and she felt a rush of panic. Who knew what he would say?

"Something about this amuses you?" Dante said coldly.

Ferrantes smiled. "Everything about this amuses me, *senhor*, including this touching scene of reunion." Ferrantes cocked his head. "I only wonder…how well do you know the *senhorita?*"

"Dante," Gabriella said quickly, "listen to me…"

Ferrantes stepped forward, elbowing another man aside. "I ask," he said softly, "because I know her well." Gabriella gasped as he wrapped a thick arm around her waist and tugged her to his side. "Intimately, one might say. Isn't that correct, Gabriella?"

Dante's eyes went cold and flat. They locked on Ferrantes's face even as he directed his question to her.

"What is he talking about?"

She had heard him use that tone before, not long after they'd met. They'd been strolling along a street in Soho. It was late, after midnight, and they'd heard a thin cry down a dark alley, the thump of something hitting the ground.

"Stay here," Dante had told her.

It had been a command, not a request, and she'd obeyed it instinctively, standing where he'd left her, hearing scuffling sounds and then thuds until she'd said to hell with obedience. She'd run toward the alley just as Dante had reappeared with an old man shuffling beside him. A street person, from the looks of him, saying "Thank you, sir," over and over, and then she'd looked at Dante, saw that his suit coat was torn, his jaw was already swelling…saw the look in his eyes that said he had done what he'd had to do…

And had enjoyed it.

"Gabriella, what is he talking about? Answer me!"

She opened her mouth. Shut it again. What could she possibly tell him? Not the truth. Never that. Never, ever that!

"Perhaps I can help, *senhor*." It was the lawyer, looking from one man to the other and smiling nervously. "Obviously, you and the *senhorita* have met before. In the States, I assume."

"*Senhor* de Souza," Gabriella said, "I beg you—"

"You could say that," Dante growled, his eyes never leaving the big man who still stood with his arm around Gabriella. Her face was as white as paper. She was trembling. Why didn't she step away from the greasy son of a bitch? Why didn't she call him a liar? No way would she have given herself to someone like this.

"In that case," the lawyer said, "you probably knew her as Gabriella Reyes."

Dante folded his arms over his chest. "Of course I know her as—"

"Her true name, her full name, is Gabriella Reyes

Viera." De Souza paused. "She is the daughter of Juan Viera."

Dante looked at him. "I thought Viera had only one child. A son."

"He had a son and a daughter." De Souza paused, delicately cleared his throat. "Ah, perhaps—perhaps we should discuss this in private, *Senhor* Orsini, yes?"

"Indeed you should," Ferrantes snarled. "There is an auction taking place here, *advogado,* or have you forgotten?"

"Let me get this straight," Dante said, ignoring him, his attention only on the attorney. "The ranch, which should be Gabriella's, will be sold to the highest bidder?"

"To me," Ferrantes looked down at Gabriella. The meaty hand that rested at her waist rose slowly, deliberately, until it lay just beneath her breast. "*Everything* will be sold to me. So you see, American, you are wrong. There is no business here for you, whatsoever."

Dante looked at him. Looked at Gabriella. Something was very wrong here. He had no idea what it was, no time to find out. He could only act on instinct, as he had done so many times in his life.

He took a deep breath, looked at the auctioneer. "What was the last bid?"

The auctioneer swallowed. "*Senhor* Ferrantes bid two hundred thousand United States dollars."

Dante nodded. "Four hundred thousand."

The crowd gasped. Ferrantes narrowed his eyes. "Six."

Dante looked at Gabriella. What had happened to her? She was as beautiful as in the past, but she had lost weight. Her eyes were enormous in the weary planes of her face. And though she was tolerating Ferrantes's touch, he could almost see her drawing into herself as if she could somehow stand within the man's embrace and yet remain apart from it.

"Gabriella," he said quietly. "I can buy this place for you."

The crowd stirred. Ferrantes's face darkened, but Dante had eyes only for the woman who had once been his lover.

"No strings," he said. "I'll buy it, sign it over to you and that'll be the end of it."

She stared at him. He could see her weighing her choices but, dammit, what was there to weigh?

"Gabriella," he said, urgency in his tone, "tell me what you want."

Ferrantes pushed Gabriella aside, took a menacing step forward. "You think you can walk in here and do anything you want, American?"

Dante ignored him. "Talk to me, Gabriella."

She almost laughed. Talk? It was too late for that. They should have talked that terrible day when her life had changed forever. She had been so alone, so frightened, so in need of her lover's strength and comfort. She'd phoned his office, found out he was away. He had not told her that. She saw it as a bad sign, but when he called the next evening and said he was back and wanted to see her, her heart had lifted. And that night, when he said he had something to tell her, she'd been sure fate had answered her plea, that he was going to say that he had gone away not to put distance between them but to think about her and now he knew, knew what he felt…

But what he had felt was that he was tired of her.

She would never forget the small blue box. The exquisite, obscenely expensive earrings. And his oh-so-polite little speech including that guilt-driven assurance that if she ever needed anything, she had only to ask.

The pain of his rejection had been momentarily dulled

by his sheer arrogance. She could not have imagined ever wanting anything from him.

But the world and her life had changed.

"The *fazenda* is mine," Ferrantes growled, "as is the woman."

Gabriella dragged a steadying breath into her lungs. "*Sim*. Please. Buy…buy the *fazenda* for me." Her words were rushed and desperate. "I will pay you back. It will take time but I'll repay every dollar."

Dante never hesitated.

"Five million dollars," he called out. "Five million, U.S."

The crowd gasped. Ferrantes cursed. The auctioneer swung his gavel.

And Dante took Gabriella in his arms and kissed her.

CHAPTER THREE

DANTE'S kiss was the last thing Gabriella expected.

The last thing she wanted.

Once, his kisses had meant everything. Tender, they'd been soft enough to bring her to the verge of tears; passionate, they'd made her dizzy and hungry for more.

And it hadn't been only his kisses that meant everything. It was the man.

Deep inside, she'd known it had not been the same for him. She'd never been foolish enough to think it was. He was rich, powerful, incredibly good-looking. Many of the models she knew dated such men. She never had...

Until him.

His initial interest had been flattering. Exciting. She had thought, *Why not?* She'd promised herself dating him would be nothing serious.

And then, despite everything, she had fallen in love with him. Deeply, desperately in love.

Dante had been magic.

But the magic was gone, lost in the cold reality of the past year. Completely gone, she told herself frantically, when she saw the sudden darkening of his eyes, the tightening of skin over bone, the all-too-familiar signs that said he was going to take her in his arms.

"Don't," she said, slapping her hands against his chest, but he was not listening, he was not listening…

"Gabriella," he murmured, saying her name softly as he used to when they made love. His arms tightened around her, he drew her against him…

And kissed her.

The room spun. The crowd disappeared. All that mattered was the sweetness of his kiss, the hardness of his body, the strength of his arms. Her foolish, desperate heart began to race.

"Dante," she whispered. The hands that had tried to push him away rose and slid up his chest, skimmed the steady beat of his heart and curved around his neck. She rose on her toes, leaned into him, parted her lips to his just as she'd done in the past.

She felt him shudder with desire at her touch.

He wanted her, still.

Wanted her as if nothing had ever separated them.

The realization shot through her like a drug, and when he groaned, thrust one hand into her hair, slid the other to the base of her spine and angled his lips over hers, his kiss going from sweet to passionate as if they were alone, alone in that perfect world his lovemaking had always created, a world in which he had never abandoned her…

A meaty hand clamped down on her shoulder, fingers biting hard into her flesh.

"Pirhana!"

The foul Portuguese curse word was followed by a stream of profanities. Her eyes flew open as Ferrantes yanked her out of Dante's arms, a stream of words even worse than *whore* flying from his lips.

Dante shot into action, grabbed Ferrantes's arm, twisted and jerked it high behind the man's back. Ferrantes hissed with fury and pain.

"I will kill you, Orsini," he said, spittle flying from his lips.

"Dante," Gabriella said desperately, "Dante, please. He'll hurt you!"

Dante pushed her behind him and brought his lips close to Ferrantes's ear.

"Touch her again," he snarled, "and I promise, you bastard, I'll be the one doing the killing!"

"She is a witch! She makes a fool of you. That you do not see it— Ahh!"

The big man yelped; his face contorted with pain as Dante forced his arm even higher.

"Listen to me, Ferrantes. You are not to speak to her. You are not to speak of her. You are not to so much as look at her or so help me God, you're a dead man!"

Dante was dimly aware of the room emptying, men rushing for the door, footsteps hurrying across the veranda, truck and car engines roaring to life outside, but he never took his eyes from Ferrantes.

"You hear me? You're to keep away from her. You got that?"

The big man's breathing was heavy. At last he gave a quick jerk of his head in assent.

Dante let go, took a step back, and Ferrantes spun around and swung at him. His hand was the size of a ham but there had been many things to learn in the wilds of Alaska, including how to defend yourself in some of the roughest bars in the world. Dante danced back; Ferrantes's fist sailed harmlessly by his face and when the big man came at him again he grunted, balled his own fist and jabbed it into the man's solar plexus with the force of a piston.

Ferrantes went down like a felled tree.

Dante stood over him for a long moment. Then he looked up, saw de Souza, saw the auctioneer…

But Gabriella was gone.

De Souza was staring at the motionless hulk on the floor as if it were a rodent. Dante grabbed him by the shoulders.

"Where is she?" he demanded.

De Souza gulped, looked from Ferrantes to Dante. "You have made a bad enemy, *senhor.*"

"Answer the question, man. Where is Gabriella?"

The *advogado* shrugged. "She is gone."

"I can see that for myself. Where?"

De Souza licked his lips. "Listen to me, *Senhor* Orsini. This situation is—how do you say—more complicated than it might at first seem."

Dante barked a laugh. "You think?" His eyes fixed on the lawyer's. "Where did she go?" he demanded. "Upstairs?"

"Not there," de Souza said quickly. He gave another expressive shrug. "She fled with the others."

Dante ran from the house. Only three vehicles remained in the clearing: his, a gold Caddy he figured was the lawyer's and the big, ugly black SUV that surely belonged to Ferrantes.

He sagged against the veranda railing.

Gabriella was gone.

And maybe that was just as well.

He'd come here to buy this place for his father. Instead, he'd bought it for a woman who had once meant something to him but no longer did. Yes, he'd kissed her. And, yes, that one kiss had damned near consumed him, but so what?

He was a normal, healthy male. She was a beautiful woman. They had a shared history. But that was it.

He looked around him at the weed-choked corral, the

dilapidated outbuildings. He'd dropped five million bucks on this place—his money, not Cesare's—but so what? The truth was he had a lot of money. An obscene amount of money, and he'd made every penny on his own. Losing five million dollars was nothing. And Gabriella didn't owe him anything. Hadn't he promised her there would be no strings? Hadn't buying the *fazenda* for her been his idea?

A muscle in Dante's jaw began to tick.

It had been his idea…hadn't it?

Yes. It damned well had. Still, he had the right to a couple of minutes of conversation. Okay, questions, not conversation, but he was entitled to ask them. Why had she returned to Brazil? Why did she want this rundown disaster? Why did it belong to the bank?

Most of all, why would an ugly SOB like Ferrantes act as if he had a claim on her?

The muscle ticked again.

And then there was the biggest question of all. Why had she melted in his arms when he'd kissed her? Hell, why had he kissed her in the first place? Forget the history thing. He was a man who never looked back—

"Yo, American!" Ferrantes stepped out of the house. He was grinning, even though his gut had to be aching. "You throw a good punch, for a Yankee."

Dante's lips drew back from his teeth. "My pleasure."

The other man chuckled. "The pleasure is all mine, Orsini. Your blow gave me the chance to think. That two intelligent men would have fought over such a woman…"

Dante narrowed his eyes. "Didn't you learn anything?" he said, his tone soft and dangerous. "I told you to watch your mouth!"

The big man lifted his hands in mock surrender. "Trust me, *meu amigo*. The woman is all yours." A sly smirk lifted one corner of his mouth. "But I must be honest. You saved me from wasting a lot of money."

Dante folded his arms. "Glad to have been of service."

"And from wasting the rest of my life."

What in hell was the man talking about?

"So, *senhor,* now I owe you a favor." Ferrantes made a show of looking around, then lowered his voice. "Before you get in too deep, ask the lady a question."

"Listen, pal, when I need advice from you—"

"Or ask the *advogado.* Perhaps he will tell you what you need to know about his charming client."

A coldness danced along Dante's spine. *Don't fall for it,* he told himself, but it was impossible to ignore the bait.

"What in hell are you talking about?"

All pretence at camaraderie vanished from Andre Ferrantes's ugly face.

"Ask de Souza whose bed your Gabriella has been sleeping in," he said coldly, "until you showed up and she decided it might be more profitable to sleep in yours."

He'd wanted to go for Ferrantes's throat, but pride held him back.

Why give the man even a small victory? Dante thought hours later, as he sped along a narrow road that led deeper and deeper into a verdant wilderness.

Bad enough she'd played him for a fool in front of everybody, including the lawyer, who'd known her game all along, and the auctioneer, who was probably still celebrating the haul he'd made. Bad enough, too, that every man in that room knew she'd slept with Ferrantes.

Not that he gave a damn that she'd been with someone else—he had no claims on her anymore—but Ferrantes? She'd wanted the ranch badly enough to lie beneath a pig like that? Open herself to him, take him deep inside her, beg him to touch her, taste her, take her… .

Dante's hands tightened on the steering wheel.

She'd done all the things with Ferrantes she had once done with him—and then he'd come along and she'd seen an easy way to put the bastard out of her life.

His mouth twisted.

What a piece of work she was! The earrings he'd bought her had been worth a small fortune but she'd made it seem as if she were too good to accept such an expensive gift from a lover. A former lover, okay, but that wasn't the point.

Apparently, accepting a ranch was different.

The car hit a pothole and swerved to the right. Dante cursed and fought the wheel, brought the car back on the road.

No wonder Ferrantes had stood there with that slab of beef he called an arm wrapped around Gabriella's waist. No wonder he'd objected when Dante kissed her. Gone crazy when she'd kissed him back.

Except, she hadn't.

He knew that now. It had all been a carefully calculated performance. The lady had seen her chance to get possession of those useless acres without continuing to spread her legs for Ferrantes.

An image, so hot and erotic it all but obliterated his vision, filled Dante's mind.

"Dammit," he snarled, and pushed the gas pedal the last inch to the floor.

The car rocketed ahead.

What an idiot he'd been! Falling for her act. Behaving precisely as she'd intended so that now he owned a useless piece of dirt in the middle of nowhere, every stinking weed, every collapsing outbuilding all his. He'd written a check for the auctioneer, ignored the man's outstretched hand, brushed past the lawyer without a word because they'd both known what was happening. They could have told him. Warned him.

Warned him?

The auctioneer's job was to sell the ranch. The lawyer's was to protect his client. Besides, de Souza had tried. *There is more to this than you know,* Senhor, he'd said. Something like that and Dante had chosen to ignore—

Something raced across the road, came to a dead stop, glared at him through eyes that were a shocking red against the dark onset of night. Dante stood on the brakes, fought to control the steering. The car swerved, spun; the tires squealed as if in pain. A wall of thick trees reared up ahead and he cursed, hung on to the steering wheel…

The car came to a shuddering halt.

The sound of the engine died. Silence and the night closed in as he sat behind the wheel breathing hard, hands shaking.

The car had done a one-eighty, ending up pointing in the direction from which he'd come.

He looked in the rearview mirror. The road behind him, what had moments ago been the road *ahead* of him, was empty. The animal—a big cat, he was almost certain—was gone.

His heart was still pounding. He took half a dozen breaths, sat back until his hands were steady again.

All this crap, reliving the stupid things he'd done almost as soon as he'd stepped off the plane at Campo Grande, was not getting him anywhere. What was done, was done. It was something he had learned to live by, how he had gone from almost flunking out of high school to doing okay in college and then putting in those years in Alaska before finally admitting that success in life wasn't such a bad thing, after all.

Besides, he was the one who'd get the last laugh.

Sure, he'd been conned into dropping a big chunk of change buying property he didn't want for a woman who meant nothing to him, but this wasn't over. As he'd walked past de Souza, the lawyer had put out his hand.

"*Senhor* Orsini?" he'd said politely. "I will expect your phone call."

Dante had looked at him blankly. De Souza had cleared his throat.

"To make an appointment to come to my office, yes? To transfer ownership of Viera y Filho to *Senhorita* Reyes."

"Yeah," he'd said brusquely, as he'd brushed by the man.

Now, Dante smiled.

Why would he transfer the deed to Gabriella?

She'd wasted her time. No way would he give her the ranch. He'd sell it to the first buyer that wanted it. Or let it go on rotting until every last sign of it had been swallowed up by the surrounding scrub. He would do whatever it took to keep her from profiting from what she'd done to him.

Still smiling, he turned the key. The engine coughed, then caught, and he headed for Bonito.

The drive, even the near accident, had done him some good. Cleared his head. He felt a thousand times better, calm and in control, and that was important.

He was a man who prided himself on being in control.

Goodbye and good riddance to this place, this cast of characters. He was going home.

By the time he reached the main road, he was whistling. He felt good. He'd get to the hotel, shower, change, phone down for room service—or no, why do that? The travel agent had faxed him a list of restaurants and bars. This was

Brazil and even in a town that specialized in eco-friendly tours, there was sure to be a hot night scene, and Brazilian women were spectacularly beautiful.

A little rest and relaxation was what he needed.

He didn't just feel good, he felt great…

Until he approached the road that led to the Viera y Filho *fazenda* and saw distant lights blazing like the fires of hell against the black night sky at the end of that road.

His good mood disappeared.

Lights. There was someone in the house. And he knew, instinctively, that someone was Gabriella. De Souza had deliberately misled him. Gabriella hadn't gone out the door, she'd gone up the stairs.

The rage he'd fought for so many hours reached out, all but consumed him. To hell with heading back to the States without confronting her. No matter what he told himself, he'd be leaving with his tail between his legs.

No way, he thought grimly. Not him.

Dante made a sharp left and headed for Gabriella.

CHAPTER FOUR

GABRIELLA came slowly down the stairs, exhausted at the end of the long day.

At least the house was quiet. Yara had left; she had her own responsibilities.

Just as well. Gabriella wanted to be alone. There were memories in this house, some bad but a few that were good; she could, at least, gather them to her tonight.

She went from room to room, switching on the lights. She'd been up since before dawn. There was nothing she could do to restore the property from the years of neglect it had suffered, but she'd done what she could inside the house, cleaning and polishing as if for company, ridiculous when the only people who had been coming were those who had wanted to take it from her.

The bank's representative. The auctioneer. Her attorney, who kept patting her on the shoulder and saying how sorry he was, yet never finding a single way to help her.

And Andre Ferrantes.

She shuddered.

Just thinking of Ferrantes sent a chill through her. He'd turned up, too. No surprise there. He'd sniffed after her like a wolf on a blood trail ever since she'd returned to the *fazenda*. Lots of sympathetic words. Lots of tsk-tsking. Lots of deep sighs.

But none of those things ever disguised the avaricious glint in his tiny eyes or the way he ran his tongue over his fleshy wet lips when he looked at her.

Today he'd finally made his move. Put his thick arm around her, his way of announcing his intentions to the world, that when he bought the ranch, she would be part of the furnishings.

Never, she thought grimly, plucking a throw pillow from the sofa and all but beating it into shape. No matter how badly she wanted this land, this house, no matter what the reasons, she'd sooner live on the streets than be in Ferrantes's debt or, even worse, his bed.

The thought was enough to make her feel ill.

And then, the miracle. The second miracle, because the first had been hearing Dante's voice, discovering him in the room, tall and imposing, hard-faced and intent. For an instant she'd imagined he'd come for her. Searched for her, found her, wanted her again.

Gabriella wrapped her arms around the pillow and shut her eyes.

Stupid thoughts, all of them.

He was here, that was all. She still didn't know why he'd come; she only knew it had nothing to do with her. But his coming had still saved her. He'd bought the *fazenda*. For her. At least, that was what he'd said.

So far, that had not happened.

He had not gone to the *advogado*'s office to sign the documents de Souza said he would have to sign for the transfer of ownership. Instead he had vanished.

The lawyer had no idea where.

"Perhaps he returned to New York," de Souza told her, shrugging his shoulders. "I do not know, *Senhorita*. I have not heard from him. I know only that he spoke with *Senhor* Ferrantes after their, ah, their disagreement."

Gabriella tossed the pillow aside.

Disagreement? She almost laughed. Was that what you called it when two men went at each other with blood in their eyes? She had fled then, terrified of the consequences, of Ferrantes winning the fight...

Of the noise of it traveling up the stairs.

So she'd gone up to the rooms that were hers, stayed there until de Souza called her name. Everyone was gone, he'd told her, including the *senhor* from the United States.

"How did—how did the fight end?" she'd asked in a shaky voice.

"*Senhor* Orsini won," the lawyer had replied with a little smile. Then his expression had sobered. "But he and Ferrantes had a private talk after. When it was done, the *senhor* drove away very fast."

Without arranging to sign transfer papers. Without doing anything to fulfill that "no strings" promise.

Why? The question plagued her through the ensuing hours. She'd come at it from a dozen different angles but she still had no answer, only the nagging worry that though Dante's initial intent had been decent, his machismo had gotten in the way.

That kiss.

The way he'd held her. Plundered her mouth. As if no time had passed since they'd been lovers. As if he still owned her. Not that he ever had, but that was the way he'd acted when they were together, as if she belonged to him even though she'd known he had no wish to belong to her.

Had it all been an act for Ferrantes? The kiss? The outrageous bid? The promise? The questions were endless, but the one that mattered most was the one she'd posed to de Souza.

"What do we do now?" she'd said.

That had earned her another little smile.

"We wait to hear from *Senhor* Orsini, of course." The smile had turned sly. "It is good to have such a powerful man as a friend, yes?"

The way he'd said "friend" had made her want to slap his face.

But she hadn't.

She knew how things looked. Dante had kissed her and she had responded, but so what? It was a simple matter of hormones and he was an expert at making her hormones respond. Besides, he'd caught her by surprise. She had never expected to see him again, never wanted to see him again. He meant nothing to her; he never had. It had taken her a while to figure that out—his easy disposal of her had wounded her pride, that was all.

She was over him. Completely over him, and—

What was that?

Gabriella threw up her hand. Lights blazing through the front windows from a fast-moving vehicle all but blinded her.

Her heart began to gallop.

"Ferrantes," she whispered. It had to be him, hot with fury. Dante had made a fool of him in front of everyone, and, he would surely think, so had she.

Tires squealed. A car door slammed. Footsteps pounded up the steps to the veranda and a hand stabbed at the doorbell, over and over and over.

Her mind raced.

What should she do? Phone the *policia?* The nearest station was miles away. Besides, would they give a damn? Ferrantes was of this place. She was not. Not anymore. Her father had seen to that. He'd told endless lies about her, turned her into an outsider...

The bell was still ringing and now the sound of a fist pounding on the door added to the din. She could not let this continue. It was too much, far too much, and she gave one last frantic look up the stairs before she took a deep breath, went to the door and flung it open.

But it wasn't Ferrantes filling the night with his presence.

It was Dante. And even as her traitorous heart lifted at the sight of him, the expression on his face made the breath catch in her throat.

Dante saw a rush of emotions flash across Gabriella's face.

Surprise. Shock. Fear. And, just before that, something he couldn't identify. Not that it mattered. Whatever she felt was meaningless compared to his rage.

She was good, though. He could almost see her clamp the lid on all the things she'd felt on seeing him again.

"Dante," she said, as politely as a capable hostess greeting a not-so-welcome drop-in guest. "I didn't expect to see you tonight."

"I'll bet you didn't."

"In fact, I thought—*Senhor* de Souza and I both thought—you'd gone back to New York."

"Without signing over the deed?"

She could almost see the sneer on his face. *Don't react to it,* she told herself, and forced a calm response.

"I only meant—"

"Trust me, sweetheart. I know exactly what you meant." He smiled; he could feel the pressure of his lips drawing back from his teeth. "Aren't you going to ask me in?"

She hesitated. He couldn't blame her. She was far from stupid.

"Actually, it's rather late."

"It's the shank of the evening. Back home, you and I would be heading out for a late supper right about now."

She flushed. "That was a long time ago."

"Supper," he said, as if she hadn't spoken, "and then maybe a stop at one of those little clubs way downtown that you liked so much."

"You liked them," she said stiffly, "I preferred simpler places."

He felt a stir of anticipation in his blood. Her accent had just thickened. She had only the slightest accent. She'd told him once, in a rare moment when they'd talked about their lives, that she'd been tutored in English from childhood—but her accent always grew more pronounced when she was trying to contain her emotions.

In bed, for example.

When they'd been making love. Her whispered words would take on the soft sounds of her native tongue. Sometimes she'd say things to him in Portuguese. Things he had not understood but his body, his mouth, his hands had known their meaning.

He looked down at her, his muscles tense.

"But you liked what we did when we went back to your apartment or mine," he said, his voice low and rough. "What we did in bed."

Her color deepened. Or maybe the rest of her face turned pale. He didn't give a damn. If she thought she was going to control the situation the way she'd controlled it this morning, she was in for a hell of a surprise.

She took a deep breath that lifted her breasts. They seemed larger than in the past. Fuller. But then, he hadn't seen her breasts in a very long time.

Too long, he thought, and a surge of hot lust rolled deep in his belly.

Lust? For a woman with no makeup on her face? A

woman wearing a loose cotton top over baggy jeans? Hell, she looked beautiful anyway, though he had never seen her dressed like this before. She'd always worn chic designer clothes when they were together. Her own clothes, though he'd often tried to buy things for her.

"I prefer to pay for my own things," she'd always said with a polite smile. She'd used that same line when he tried to buy her any but the simplest of gifts.

She didn't need convincing anymore, he thought coldly. She hadn't blinked an eye at his dropping five million bucks on her this morning.

"Whatever we did in New York is over, *senhor.*"

"Such formality, sweetheart. After all we've been to each other?"

"The past," she said stiffly, ignoring his remark, "has no bearing on this matter."

"But it does," he said softly. "After all, I bought this house today."

She nodded, folded her arms over her breasts. "Yes. And…and it was a very kind thing for you to—"

"Based on the way you looked at your boyfriend, I have to assume you were glad I did."

"*Sim.* I was. But Ferrantes is not—"

"Your lover." He shrugged his shoulders. "Whatever you want to call him."

He watched the tip of her tongue peep out, watched it sweep across her lips and hated himself for the way it made him feel, hated her for doing it. It was deliberate; everything she'd done from the second she'd set eyes on him this morning had been deliberate.

"Must have been hell, a woman as fastidious as you, sleeping with a man like—"

She slapped him. Her hand moved so fast he never really saw the blow coming. The best he could do was jerk back, grab her wrist, twist it behind her as he tugged her toward him.

"What's the matter, baby? Does the truth hurt?"

"Get out," she hissed. "Get out of my house!"

"This isn't your house. Not anymore."

Tears filled her eyes. Angry tears, phony tears. One of the two. He knew damned well they couldn't be any other kind.

"I bought it. Just as you assumed I would."

She looked at him as if he'd lost his mind. "Assumed?" A choked laugh burst from her throat. "I didn't even know you were in Brazil! Come to think of it, why *are* you in my country?"

"Don't flatter yourself, sweetheart. I didn't come looking for you."

She knew that. Still, hearing it hurt. It was time to hurt him back.

"I came on business. Family business."

"Ah, yes," she said, tossing her head. "The famous *famiglia* Orsini. How could I have forgotten?"

She gasped as his hold on her tightened. In the few months they'd been together, they had never discussed his family, his father's underworld connections. She'd have known about it, of course. That the Orsini brothers were sons of Cesare Orsini was favorite gossip-column fodder.

"What's that supposed to mean?"

"Only that perhaps the apple doesn't fall far from the tree. Dammit, you're hurting me!"

She was twisting against his hand, trying to get free, but each jerk of her body only brought her more closely against him.

It was agony.

Exquisite agony.

The soft brush of her breasts against the hardness of his

chest. The whisper of her belly against his. The feel of her thighs rubbing lightly over his. Just the sight of her, all that sun-streaked hair tumbling around her face, that lush mouth, the eyes deep enough for a man to get lost in.

Memories swept through him.

The feel of her, moving beneath him.

The scent of her, when he brought her to climax.

The taste of her mouth, her skin, her clitoris.

Desire, wild, hot and dangerous, took fire. It thickened his blood, ignited nerve endings, brought him to full, rampant arousal. Maybe she was right. Maybe the apple didn't fall far from the tree. Go back a couple of generations, to the land of his ancestors, a woman would not have dared make a fool of an Orsini as this woman had done this morning.

On a low growl, Dante clasped Gabriella's shoulders, lifted her to him and claimed her mouth.

She fought. It didn't matter. Kissing her, subduing her, taking her was everything.

This morning she had told him what she wanted. Now, it was his turn to tell her what he wanted.

Her. Her, in his bed, again. For as long as he chose to keep her there. He'd never wanted another man's leavings but this—this was different.

He would wipe Ferrantes's possession away. Replace it with his own demands. His own pleasure. Her pleasure, too, because that would happen, she would soften under his touch as she had earlier today, she would moan against his lips, run her hands up his chest, press herself to him, yes, as she was doing now, moving her hips against his, making those sexy little whimpers that could raise the temperature a hundred degrees.

He groaned her name. Slid his hands under her bulky shirt. Cupped her breasts and groaned again at the feel of them in his hands, all warm, sweet silky flesh straining against her bra, filling his palms, the nipples lifting to the caressing sweep of his thumbs.

"Gabriella," he said, his voice urgent, and she wound her arms around his neck, sucked his tongue into the heat of her mouth…

Merda! What in hell was he doing?

Cursing, he pushed her from him. She stumbled back, shoulders hitting the wall, eyes flying open and fixing on his. She looked shocked, on the verge of tears, but he wasn't fooled. He was letting her do it all over again, blinding him to reality, using sex to turn his body on and his brain off as if she were a sorceress and he a fool she could enchant.

But he wasn't.

"Nice," he said, as if he'd been in control all the time. "Very nice. We're going to get along just fine."

"Get out," she said, her voice trembling.

"Come on, sweetheart. Don't take it so hard. And, what the hell, it'll be easier with me than it was with Ferrantes, we both know that."

She swung at him again but he was ready this time. He caught her hand, dragged her against him.

"You said—you said you would give my home to me. No strings, you said."

"That was before I knew you'd already made a deal with good old Andre."

She spat a word at him and he laughed. Turned out, some obscenities sounded pretty much the same whether they were said in the Sicilian of his youth or the Portuguese of hers.

"You think this is amusing?"

Dante lowered his head until his eyes were almost even with hers.

"What I think," he said in a cold whisper, "is that you get to have a choice."

"What is that supposed to mean?"

"It means I'll sell the place to Ferrantes in the blink of an eye."

"He wouldn't pay five million dollars."

"My accountant keeps telling me I can use a couple more nonperforming assets."

Her mouth trembled. Her eyes filled. It was hard not to feel sorry for her. Hard—but not impossible.

"I hate you, Dante Orsini!"

"I guess the question is, who do you hate more? Me or Ferrantes? Of course, you can always turn us both down. Pack up, move out—"

A thin cry drifted into the room. Gabriella stiffened, jerked back in his arms.

"What's that?"

"A…a fox," she said quickly.

She was lying. He could see it in her face. The cry came again. Dante narrowed his eyes.

"A fox in the house?"

"A monkey, then," Gabriella said, rushing the words together. "Sometimes they get into the attic."

The hell it was. You didn't have to grow up in the country to know whatever was making that sound was not a monkey or a fox. Dante thrust her aside and started for the stairs. She ran in front of him and held out her hands.

"Get out of my way," he growled.

"Dante. Please. Just leave. I'll pack tonight. I'll be out by morning. I promise—"

He lifted her as if she were a feather, set her aside, took the stairs two at a time, following what were now steady sobs down a long hall, through an open door, into a softly lit room…

And saw a crib, a blue blanket, a blue teddy bear…

And a baby, kicking its arms and legs and sobbing its heart out.

Dante stopped on a dime. Gabriella rushed past him and lifted the child into her arms. *Say something,* Dante thought furiously…but no words would come. He didn't seem capable of anything besides looking at her and at the baby.

"Meu querido," she crooned, "dearest one, don't cry!"

The baby's cries changed to sad little hiccups; Gabriella held the small body against her so that the baby's face was against her shoulder. A pair of eyes—pale-blue eyes fringed by long, dark lashes—peered at Dante.

The room filled with silence. After a very long time, Dante cleared his throat.

"Yours?" It was not a brilliant comment but it was all he could think of saying.

Gabriella looked at him. He could read nothing in her face.

"I said, is the child—"

"I heard your question." Her eyes were bright with what he could only assume was defiance. "Yes. The child is mine."

He felt as if someone had dropped a weight onto his heart.

"Yours," he said thickly. "And Ferrantes's."

Gabriella made a choked sound, neither a laugh or a sob, then lowered her face to the baby's. Dante stared at her. At the child. He knew he should say something…or maybe he should just smash his fist through the wall.

He did neither. If life lesson number one was that what was over was over, number two was the importance of maintaining self-control.

Dante turned and walked out.

CHAPTER FIVE

HE DROVE like a man possessed by demons, a hot fist of rage twisting in his belly.

That Gabriella should have slept with a pig like Ferrantes, that she'd carried his child in her womb…

Dante slammed the heel of his hand against the steering wheel.

"Come on," he muttered, "come on, dammit!" Couldn't this freaking car go any faster? He couldn't wait to get back to the hotel, toss his stuff in his suitcase and get the hell out of Brazil.

He had to phone his old man eventually, but what would he tell him? That he'd gotten it all wrong, there was no dissolute Viera son inheriting the ranch…

Only a dissolute daughter.

A woman who'd warmed his bed every night for, what, a few weeks? Okay. For three months. He'd taken her the first night they'd gone out, in an explosion of mutual passion like nothing he'd ever known before, taken her night after night, and the intensity of that passion had never diminished, not even when it had begun a subtle change to something he hadn't been able to define except to know that it made him uncomfortable.

Was that the reason he'd ended their affair?

Not that it mattered. There were more important things to consider.

Like what in hell he was going to do with a ranch.

He'd bought it for a woman who'd never existed, a woman who'd walked away from him and never looked back, who'd gone from his arms to another's without missing a beat, and who gave a damn? God knew, he hadn't been celibate these past months. There'd been a parade of women in and out of his life. So what if there'd been a parade of men in and out of hers?

What mattered now was that he was stuck with five million bucks' worth of absolutely nothing.

He'd been scammed, and scammed good—and now he was the unfortunate owner of a place he didn't want, all his until he could unload it.

Note to self, Dante thought grimly. Phone de Souza. Instruct him to sell the *fazenda* and never mind the price. Forget how much money he'd lose on the deal. Just find a buyer, he'd say. Any buyer and, yeah, that included Ferrantes. In fact, selling the ranch to Ferrantes was a great idea.

Until he'd shown up, Gabriella had been more than willing to pay the price Ferrantes demanded. She could damned well go on paying it now.

He wasn't the Sir Galahad type. Sir Stupid, was more like it, a Don Quixote tilting at windmills. Well, that was over. Yeah, definitely, let Ferrantes buy the damned ranch. It was what Gabriella deserved, the perfect payback. Let her spend the next hundred years in the pig's bed. It didn't matter to him. She was just someone he'd been with for a while.

Nothing special. Just like seeing her with another man's kid was nothing special...

A kid with a solemn expression and pale-blue eyes.

Dante cursed and pulled onto the shoulder of the road, put the engine in neutral and sat gripping the steering wheel hard enough to turn his knuckles white.

You could put what he knew about kids in a teacup and have room left. Why would he know anything about them? His brothers, his sisters, were all unmarried. If the guys he played touch football with Sundays in Central Park had kids, he never saw them. Children were aliens from a planet he'd never had any interest in inhabiting.

The only children he ever saw were being pushed through the park in strollers. And, yeah, there were people with kids living in his condo building, now that he thought about it. Like a woman he'd met in the lobby a couple of weeks ago. He'd been heading out, so had she, both of them waiting for taxis in a driving rainstorm, except she'd had a pink-swathed bundle in her arms.

"Nasty weather," he'd said, because she'd kept looking at him as if she expected him to make conversation.

"Uh-huh," she'd replied, but she'd seemed to be waiting for something more. Finally he'd caught on.

"Cute," he'd said, nodding at the bundle. It wasn't. Not particularly. It was just a baby, but evidently he'd said the right thing because the mom beamed.

"Isn't she?" she'd said, and then she'd added, proudly, as if the information rated applause, "She's four months old today."

Four months.

And about the same size as the baby he'd just seen. The difference was that Gabriella's kid had those blue eyes, that solemn I'm-an-adult-in-miniature look he'd seen before....

The realization almost stole his breath away.

He saw those eyes, that expression in the mirror each morning when he shaved.

"No," he said aloud. "No! Impossible."

But it was adding up. The eyes. The expression. The dark hair. Figure the child's age at four months, add on nine more... His head did the calculations no single, unattached, contented male wanted to do and reached an inescapable possibility.

Gabriella might have become pregnant in New York. And if she had...

Dante sat back. No. He couldn't go there. All those years ago, Teresa D'Angelo's monumental lie. He'd never had sex with her, with any woman without using a condom.

Gabriella could be lying, too.

Except she hadn't lied. She hadn't said the child was his. And she'd have told him. "Dante," she'd have said, "I'm pregnant with your baby." Teresa damned well had. There were times he could still hear her voice whining that he had to marry her.

Surely, Gabriella, any woman, would have made the same demand.

Which meant, he thought, on a relieved rush of exhaled breath, which meant the kid was not his. Forget the eye color. The face. The time frame. Babies were babies. They all looked alike...

"Merda," he hissed, and he turned the key, put the car in gear, and drove back to the *fazenda* for the second time that night.

Daniel had finally fallen asleep.

He'd fussed for the last half hour. Unusual for him. He was generally an easy baby to deal with. He ate, he slept, he kicked his tiny legs, pumped his arms and grinned. The grin, especially, was a delight because his usual expression was thoughtful, almost solemn, so that when he grinned, his whole face lit.

Just like his—

Gabriella blinked. No. She was not going there. It had taken her weeks and weeks not to look at her son and see the man who'd once been her lover. She was not going to permit the events of one day to start her on that path again.

Carefully she lowered her baby into his crib, drew a light blanket to his chin, then bent and kissed his forehead, inhaling his sweet, baby scent. Her lips curved in a smile. *Deus,* how she adored her little boy. She'd been terrified when she'd realized she was carrying him. Now he was the focal point of her life.

Everything she did, she did for him.

It was why she'd wanted to save the *fazenda.*

Sighing, she turned out the light, went to her own room and undressed.

If only she could have done it. For Daniel. For his connection to a place that was in the Viera blood. And for the memory of her brother. She had loved Arturo with all her heart, just as he had loved her. No one else ever had, surely not Dante. She'd been his plaything. His toy.

And she had let him hurt her for the last time today.

Gabriella turned on the shower and stepped under the spray.

Dante was history. Her son was the future. She had to plan what she would do next, now that the ranch was truly gone. She'd harbored hope until the last minute, even though she'd known, in her heart, that the small amount of money she still possessed would not be sufficient to save it. The amount owed on it was too big. Her father had mortgaged and remortgaged the *fazenda* so often she'd lost count, frittering the money away on women, horses and cards. By the time Arturo had inherited it, the bank stood ready to foreclose.

And then, despite the doctors, the treatments, virtually all her savings from modeling, he had died.

The bank had moved in for the kill. She'd made her pathetic financial offer, they'd turned it down, and Ferrantes had come sniffing at her heels. She'd told him what he could do with his disgusting suggestions. He'd laughed and said she would change her mind after the auction. She told him she would never do that; in fact, she had not even intended to go to the auction—why break her heart even more by seeing a pig such as him take what should have been her son's inheritance?

Then she'd heard Dante's voice.

She could not have kept from going to him any more than the big, beautiful hawk moths could keep from beating themselves to death against the lit windows of the house at night.

Why had she believed he'd buy the *fazenda* for her? Worse, why had she let him kiss her? To let that happen… to give in to the kiss, to respond like a wanton to the feel of his arms, the heat of his body, the never-forgotten taste of his mouth and then to have him show how little he thought of her by believing she would have slept with Ferrantes…

That she would have slept with any man after having been with him and, *Deus,* she hated him for that, for leaving his mark on her lips, her skin, her stupid heart.

Gabriella froze.

Someone was ringing the doorbell. Banging on the door. She could hear it all the way up here, even with the water running. It would wake Daniel, but how could she let Ferrantes in?

Because, this time it would be him.

She didn't take the time to towel off. Instead, she flung on her robe, tied the sash and ran downstairs. Her heart was racing. She needed a weapon. Her father had kept guns but she didn't know where they'd be. Arturo, who'd despised killing things, had probably disposed of them.

"Gabriella! Open this door."

She blinked. Dante? Why had he returned? It couldn't be him. But when she turned on the outside lights and peered out the window, it was his rental car she saw parked before the house, not Ferrantes's obscenely extravagant SUV.

What did he want now? There was only one way to find out. She took a steadying breath and cracked the door an inch.

"I don't know why you came back," she said, or started to say. But just as he'd done a little while ago, Dante brushed past her as if she were nothing. His easy arrogance was infuriating.

A good thing, because it swept away the sudden ache in her heart the unexpected sight of him provoked.

"Excuse me," she said coldly, "but I did not invite you in. It is very late, and—"

He swung toward her, eyes bright and hard as diamonds.

"Yes," he said coldly, "it is definitely very late."

His gaze swept over her, lingering on the rise of her breasts, the length of her thighs. She thought of how the thin cotton robe must be clinging to her damp body and she flushed and folded her arms.

His smile was thin and dangerous. "Dressed for company?" he said softly.

She could feel her color deepen. "Dressed for bed," she said coolly. "My days have an early start."

His smile vanished.

"Taking care of a kid must cut down on your social life."

Her chin lifted. "What do you want?"

"It's hard to imagine a city girl like you enjoying this kind of life."

"That only shows how little you know about me."

A muscle jumped in his cheek. What was she talking about? He knew a lot about her. She preferred white wine. She didn't eat red meat. She wore clothes by big-time designers.

Those things constituted knowing a woman, didn't they? Sure they did. It meant he knew what restaurants she preferred, what to choose on a menu, what to tell his PA to buy her whenever he decided it was time to give a woman a gift.

"Dante. I asked you a question. Why did you come back? We said all we had to say an hour ago."

He dragged his thoughts together. She was wrong; they hadn't said all there was to say an hour ago and he damned well wasn't leaving this time until they had.

"That's just the point," he said slowly. "I'm not sure we did."

"What are you talking about?"

"You never answered the one question that matters."

She kept her eyes on his, but her face lost a little color. "What question?"

"Gabriella. No games." He took a step toward her; his eyes grew suddenly dark. "Is the child his?" He paused. "Or is it mine?"

His words hit her with an almost physical force. When she'd first realized she was pregnant, she'd imagined this scene endless times.

It had never ended well.

That was the reason she hadn't fallen apart that terrible night Dante had taken her to dinner and told her he didn't want her anymore, just seconds before she'd been about to tell him she was carrying his child.

He had not wanted her then. He did not want her now. So, why was he asking the question?

Better still, how should she answer it?

He came closer, close enough so she had to tilt her head back to look at him.

"It's a simple question, Gabriella. Whose kid is it?"

Her heart was pounding. His voice was hard. So was his face. Hard and threatening. What did he want? If only she knew.

His hands closed on her wrists.

"Answer the question."

Why should she tell him now? She'd gone through the worst alone. Pregnant. No longer able to model. Coming home because she had no other choice, coming home to her father's cold derision, to the illness and death of first him and then her brother.

Gabriella tossed her head, searched and found the you're-boring-me look she'd perfected for her stints on the runways of Paris, Milan and New York.

"Why ask when you already supplied the answer?"

His hands gripped her harder. She could sense the tightly controlled anger all but pouring off him.

"Answering a question with a question is a load of bull and you know it," he said grimly. "One more time. Who does the kid belong to?"

"The 'kid,' as you so charmingly put it, belongs to me. That's all you need to know. Now, get out!"

She gasped as he put a little twist on her wrists, lifted her to her toes. "Get out?" he said very softly, and flashed another of those thin, dangerous smiles. "Aren't you forgetting something, baby? This isn't your house. It's mine."

Her heart gave a thump so loud she was amazed he didn't seem to hear it.

"The *advogado*—*Senhor* de Souza said I did not have to vacate for forty-eight hours."

"You'll vacate when I say so." His mouth twisted. "You want those forty-eight hours? Tell me what I want to know."

Gabriella jerked against his grasp; he slid his hands to her shoulders, cupped them hard enough so she could feel the imprint of his fingers.

"It is none of your business."

"How old is the kid?"

"Four months. You see? I have given you an answer. Now, get—"

"Four months. And you left me a year ago."

"*I* left *you?*" She laughed. "You left me, Dante. You…you discarded me like…like a toy you'd tired of."

His mouth twisted. "I never thought of you as a toy."

"'It's been fun, Gabriella,'" she said, in uncanny imitation of his message if not his exact words, "'but it's time I moved on. There are so many women out there—'"

"I never said that," he shot back, but he could feel the color rising in his face.

"It was what you meant."

She tossed her head; her damp curls flew about her face in wild abandon.

God, she was so beautiful!

Her robe was made of cotton. It was not fashionable. It looked old, a little worn, but she made it look regal. The thin fabric clung to her body like silk, outlining her breasts, cupping them as his hands had once had the right to do. Her nipples poked against the cotton. He remembered their shape, their size, their color.

Their taste.

Sweet. Incredibly sweet. How he had loved to lick them. Suck them. Bite gently on them while she buried her hands in his hair and sobbed his name. He'd feast on her breasts until she trembled in his arms and then he'd slide his hand down, down, down until he cupped her, felt her heat, felt her body weep with need for his.

His erection was swift and almost painful. He let go of her, turned his back, strode across the room while he fought for control, furious with himself for losing it, with her for making him lose it. Seconds passed. At last he swung toward her again.

"How long do you think it will take me to get answers, Gabriella? An hour? A day? One call to my lawyer and he'll set the wheels in motion. I'll know where the kid was born—"

"Stop talking about him that way! He has a name. Daniel."

"And on his birth certificate? What's his surname?"

"Reyes," she said, lying, hating herself for the instant of weak sentimentality that had made her list Dante Orsini as her son's father.

"Fine." Dante took his mobile phone from his pocket and flipped it open.

"What are you doing?"

"Calling my attorney. You want to do this the hard way, we will. But I promise you, you're only making me even more angry than I already am." His lips twisted. "And that's not what you want. I promise you it isn't."

He was right. She knew that. He would be a formidable enemy. Besides, what would it matter if she told him the truth? Nothing. Absolutely nothing. Nothing was what she wanted from him. She had reached that decision the night he'd cast her aside.

Really, what was she protecting but her pride?

And yet…and yet he was a powerful man. A complex man. That he had returned to ask her about the baby proved it. If she admitted he was Daniel's father, anything was possible.

"Gabriella." His voice was soft but his eyes were ice. "What's it going to be? Do we do this my way—or the hard way?"

He watched her face, saw the play of emotions across it. She was shivering, from the cool of the night or from anger. He didn't give a damn. And if it was all he could do to keep from hauling her into his arms again and kissing her until she sighed his name and trembled not with cold or rage but with need, what did that prove except that she was a woman, an incredibly beautiful woman he'd never stopped wanting and—dammit, what did *that* have to do with anything?

"For the last time," he said sharply. "Is Daniel mine?"

Perhaps it was exhaustion. Perhaps it was acceptance of the inevitable. Or perhaps, Gabriella thought, perhaps it was hearing her son's name on the lips of the man who had planted his seed deep in her womb thirteen long months ago.

Whatever the reason, she knew it was time to stop fighting.

"Yes," she said wearily, "he is. So what?"

Of all the night's questions, that was the only one that mattered. And Dante knew, in that instant, his world would never be the same again.

CHAPTER SIX

GABRIELLA had promised herself she would not tell Dante that her baby was his—but that was when telling him would have meant seeking him out after Daniel's birth, and what would she have said then?

"Hello, Dante, how have you been and, by the way, here's your son?"

Logic had kept her from something so foolish. Dante didn't want her; why would he want to know she'd had his child?

But this—this was different.

Fate, circumstance, whatever, had brought him back into her life. He had seen her little boy, asked her a direct question. How could she lie to him?

Now, waiting for him to react, she realized that she *should* have lied.

He looked as if he'd been struck dumb.

If this were an old movie, if she was Meg Ryan and he was Tom Hanks, he'd have gone from shock to joy in a heartbeat. But this wasn't a movie. More to the point, this was Dante Orsini, the man who lost interest in a woman after a couple of months. She'd known his reputation—and she'd wanted him anyway. The part of her that yearned to be a sophisticate had said she could handle an affair like that.

Wrong. Agonizingly wrong. She had not been able to handle it, especially when he'd cut her from his life as if she'd never been part of it. How on earth could she have told him she'd had his child after that?

But she *had* told him now, only after he'd bullied her into submission.

No, she thought, watching him, no, this was not a movie. It was real life. And Dante's face said it all.

Shock. Disbelief. Horror. His color had drained away until the same pale-blue eyes she saw in her baby's face glittered like pools of winter ice in his.

She took a steadying breath. She wasn't feeling very well. The auction. Ferrantes. Dante turning up and now this. Her head ached. The truth was, everything ached. Maybe she was coming down with something or maybe she was simply reacting to the endless, awful day. Whatever the reason, she wanted Dante out of here. She was not up to trying to explain anything to him or to hearing him deny that Daniel was his.

But, strange as it might seem, she could understand it.

She'd been in denial, too. Complete denial. She hadn't even admitted the possibility she might be pregnant when she had missed her period. Her cycle had never been regular so she hadn't thought anything about being late. She had no morning queasiness. No tenderness in her breasts. And then one night, alone in her bed because Dante was away on business, it had simply hit her.

Maybe she was pregnant.

She'd thrown on some clothes, rushed to the all-night pharmacy on the next block, bought a home pregnancy test kit, took it home, peed on the little stick…

Two hours and six test kits later, she'd slumped to the

cold tile bathroom floor in horror. So, yes, she could see that Dante might react with shock....

"—be mine, Gabriella?"

She blinked, looked at him. His color was back. So was his arrogance. It was in his voice, in the way he was looking at her, even in the way he held himself. Aloof, removed, apart. Once, she'd found that lord-of-the-universe attitude sexy. Not anymore. She was no longer the foolish, impressionable woman who'd fallen for the great Dante Orsini.

"Did you hear me? I said, how could the child be mine?"

She felt the throbbing in her temples increase in tempo. The cold question hurt. She would not let him know that, of course. He had hurt her enough the night he'd handed her those damnable earrings.

"The usual way," she said with deliberate sarcasm. "Or did you not take Sex Ed 101?"

"This isn't the least bit amusing," he said coldly. "I used condoms. Always."

Yes, he had. Sometimes, she'd done it for him. They'd both liked that. She could remember, with heart-stopping clarity, the silk-over-steel feel of him against her palms. The feel of his hand in her hair, cupping the back of her head as she bent to him.

"Gabriella." His voice was frigid. "Did you hear what I said? You know damned well that I always used protection."

This was more than denial. He was accusing her of lying. She wanted to ball up her fist and hit him. What kind of woman did he think she was? Did he think she would make up a story such as this?

"What I know," she said, "is that I became pregnant despite your 'protection.'"

His mouth thinned. "If a condom had failed, I'd have known it."

Oh, how she wanted to slap that superior-to-thou expression off his face!

"Of course," she said with a bitter smile. "You are, after all, the man who knows everything."

"I know that it would be difficult for anyone to see how I could have impregnated you."

He sounded as if he were describing a laboratory experiment instead of the coming together of a man and a woman. Didn't he remember how sex had been between them? She did. She could remember it all. Dante, between her thighs. His mouth drinking from hers. The feel of him, slowly entering her. The scent of his skin, the essence of their shared passion....

Deus, what was the matter with her? Why had she told him Daniel was his? This discussion was without purpose. The only interest he would possibly have in her baby was in convincing himself the baby was not his.

And that was fine, she thought, and moved briskly to the door, wrapped her hand around the knob and yanked it open.

"We are done here, Dante."

"Done?" He laughed. "We haven't even started. I want answers."

"You have your answer. You asked whose child Daniel was. I told you. You denied it. We have nothing more to say to each other."

He reached out his hand, slapped the door closed and stepped closer to her. He could feel his adrenaline pumping. Did she really think she could toss him out? Never mind that he owned this house. How about the bombshell she'd just dropped on him? Telling him the kid upstairs was his....

You asked, a sly voice inside him whispered.

Yes. He'd asked. And she'd answered. He had every

right to follow up with questions—or did she assume he'd accept her fantastic claim just because she'd made it?

A man only did something that stupid once in a lifetime. He'd done a lot of growing up since the incident with Teresa D'Angelo.

"Let's assume the kid is mine."

Bile rose in her throat. "Go away," she said, her voice shaking. "Forget this conversation ever took place."

"Which is it? Are you claiming he's mine or that he isn't?"

It was too late to lie. "He is yours," she said wearily, "but only by biological accident."

"Did you know you were pregnant with the kid the night we broke up?"

"I told you," she said, her eyes suspiciously bright, "he has a name. Daniel."

"Fine. Great. Did you know you were carrying Daniel when we broke up?"

"The night you said I'd worn out my welcome, you mean?"

"Dammit, answer the question. Did you know?"

"What if I did?"

"Didn't it occur to you to tell me?"

Her eyes brightened with anger. "When? Before the earrings or after?"

He felt his face heat. She made it sound as if he'd been trying to buy her off, as if this whole damned thing was his fault.

"I gave you a gift because I…I wanted you to know you'd meant something to me."

Her hand flew through the air, connected, hard, with his cheek. He caught her wrist, dragged her arm behind her back. He knew he wasn't being gentle. She winced, rose to her toes but he didn't give a damn.

"Do not," he snarled, "do not, whatever you do, try to make it my fault you didn't inform me of this—of this situation!"

"Is that what it was?" Her voice shook. "Because I'd describe it differently. I was pregnant. Pregnant with your child. And you were dumping me and tossing me a...a bauble when all I'd ever wanted from you was...was—" She tried to jerk away but his hand only tightened on her. "Let go of me, Dante. Do us both a favor and just go away."

She was trembling.

She had trembled that night, too. He had noticed it but he'd told himself it meant nothing, that she'd get over it. She was an adult; she was a model, dammit. She'd dated a lot of men.

Hadn't she?

She'd seemed so innocent in his bed. As if everything they did, everything he did, was new to her. And that night, after he'd told her it was over, there'd been something in her eyes, a quick flash he'd chosen not to think about.

It was there now.

Was it a flash of pain?

His throat tightened.

He knew how to soothe that pain. He could gather her in his arms. Hold her against his heart. Kiss her. Caress her. Tell her that he'd never stopped thinking of her. That he'd missed her. That he still wanted her.

Merda!

What in hell was he thinking? How could she still have this effect on him? It was why he'd stopped seeing her, not because the affair had gone on too long but because he'd felt her getting inside him, getting to him. Well, it wasn't going to happen again, especially now. The last thing he needed was to react to her, feel that tug of lust low in his belly that he'd always felt when he was with her.

For all he knew, she was counting on it.

Some tears, a kiss, and he'd bought her the *fazenda*. Now this fantastic story, a few tears, another kiss and he would say, sure, the kid was his and how much would she need to keep it and herself in the style to which she so obviously wanted to grow accustomed?

Was the boy his? That was the question of the century. If the answer was yes, he'd do whatever had to be done, but he wasn't about to accept a woman's word as proof. Been there, done that, he thought grimly, and he let go of Gabriella's wrist and stepped back.

"I want proof."

"You don't need proof. I want nothing from you."

"Like you didn't want the *fazenda* when you climbed all over me this morning? Come on, baby. Let's not play games. I want proof of the kid's—of Daniel's parentage. When was he born? Where? Is my name on his birth certificate?"

Tears were streaming down her face. If this was a performance, it was a damned good one.

"Get out," she hissed. "Get out of my life! I did not ask you for anything when I carried my baby. I am not asking you for anything now. I *never* wanted anything from you, Dante! Not your money, not your fancy gifts—"

"But you wanted this," he growled, and he gave up fighting what he wanted, what he always wanted when he was near her. He swept his arms around her, bent his head and captured her mouth with his, kissing her hard, kissing her without mercy, forcing her lips apart, his tongue penetrating her, demanding the response she had always, always given him.

But she gave him nothing tonight. She stood motionless within his embrace. Slowly he raised his head. Her eyes were open, dark and empty and filled with pain.

"I beg you," she whispered. "If you ever cared for me at all, please, go away."

He stared at her. Of course he had cared for her. The truth was, he'd cared for her too much. He wanted to tell her that, to kiss her again, to hold her close and change her unhappy tears to soft, sweet sighs...

He stepped back.

What the hell had he been thinking?

The fact of it was, he *hadn't* been thinking.

He had to get out of here. Talk to his lawyer. His brothers. Arrange for tests and if the tests came up positive, figure out how to handle all of this.

He went out of the house without so much as a backward look.

One thing was certain, he told himself as he drove away.

This time, he would not turn around and go back. He was done with Gabriella. With Brazil.

There was nothing, absolutely nothing here for him.

All he could think of was getting home.

To hell with waiting for morning, he thought grimly as he strode into the lobby of his hotel. It was very late and the concierge was dozing behind his desk, but who gave a damn?

Dante woke him. Told him he wanted to rent a plane and a pilot. The concierge yawned. Dante spoke sharply. Pulled out his checkbook, said he wanted that plane, wanted it now.

A couple of calls, and it was done.

He was airborne an hour later. The plane was handsome, the pilot was efficient, the sky was shot through with moonlight and stars.

And Dante...Dante was in a mess.

He was a man who had never shirked responsibility.

Wasn't that how he'd ended up in Bonito in the first place? Because Cesare had somehow transferred responsibility for righting some long-ago wrong to him? Yes, Cesare had gotten the details wrong. There was no dying man, no successful ranch about to be dropped into the hands of a son incapable of running it. There was, instead, a ranch he'd somehow ended up owning.

Like it or not, the *fazenda* was his, not his father's.

A muscle knotted in his jaw.

And there was more.

There was a woman, alone and penniless. A baby she said was his.

Dante groaned and closed his eyes.

A mess, indeed.

What he'd said was true. He always used a condom even though, okay, there'd been times with Gabriella—and only with Gabriella—that he'd wanted to make love without that thin layer of latex sheathing him. The need to feel the slide of his erect penis against the warm silk walls of her had driven him half-crazy. He'd wanted to know that nothing, absolutely nothing separated him from her, that she was his in a way he'd never wanted another woman to be his.

"Dammit," he growled, shifting his weight in the leather seat.

Thinking X-rated thoughts gave a man's body a predictable reaction. And turning himself on was not what this was all about.

Besides, he would never have done such a stupid thing as have unprotected sex.

He enjoyed risk. Back-country skiing with the ever-present danger of avalanche. White-water kayaking. Skydiving. Letting his money and his reputation ride on financial deals that made other men blanch. He was into all that.

But sex without protection? That wasn't risk, it was suicide unless you were ready to marry, settle down, have kids. He wasn't. For all he knew, he would never be ready. He knew what women were like. They schemed. They plotted. They wanted wealthy husbands and they weren't above doing whatever it took to get them.

So, no sex without protection.

Still, accidents happened.

If you didn't leave a woman's body quickly enough, after you ejaculated, if you didn't get out and get that rubber off, there could be a problem. He'd always done it right. That one explosive moment, the sense of welcome release and then a kiss, because he knew after-play was important to a woman, a light caress, and he withdrew, headed for the john, took care of things. No wham, bam, thank you, ma'am, but no lingering so long that a rubber could leak, either.

Except…except, toward the end of things with Gabriella, he hadn't always followed those rules.

There'd been times the thought of withdrawing from all that heat, that sweet warmth, had seemed impossible. Times he'd stayed deep inside her, holding her, kissing her, not wanting to leave her even after he'd come.

How protective was a condom then?

Not very, he thought glumly. And whose fault was that, if not his own?

And, damn, even now, his body stirred at the memory.

Okay. Enough of that. The sex had been fantastic. The truth was, he'd never had better sex before or since, but that had nothing to do with this situation. And, yeah, it *was* a situation, even if she found the word offensive. And the only way to deal with it was head-on.

He took out his phone, flipped it open. Brought up his contact list. Paused, his finger above his attorney's name. Thought about the tests the guy would recommend, the time they'd take to run. Thought about Gabriella, alone with a baby in that big, falling-down house and Ferrantes salivating all over her.

Dante muttered a couple of ripe obscenities, put the phone away, rose to his feet and walked to the front of the plane. The flight attendant looked up as he made his way past her, gave him a surprised smile.

"Ah, *senhor,* you wish something? You had only to press the call button."

He ignored her, rapped sharply on the cockpit door, then opened it.

"Captain."

The pilot and copilot turned and looked at him. He saw confusion, then concern on their faces and silently called himself a fool. One did not enter an airplane cockpit, even on a chartered plane, so precipitously in today's world. That he had done so only gave proof to what he already knew: he had not settled things in Brazil, and until he did, he would not be in any condition to move on with his own life.

"Captain," he said quickly, offering what he hoped was a reassuring smile, "forgive me for intruding but I wish to change our destination."

His words only made the men look more alarmed.

"I wish to return to Bonito," he said, even more quickly. "My apologies for the inconvenience and, of course, I will pay for the flight as arranged, plus an additional amount for the change in plans."

The pilot got straight to the point.

"Because?" he said, and waited.

What was the answer that would be best understood? "A woman," Dante said briskly.

The pilot and copilot both grinned. "Ah. In that case...*no problema, Senhor* Orsini. We will be back on the ground in no time."

Dante nodded. "Excellent."

And it was excellent. He'd return to Brazil, do everything that had to be done. He'd promised Gabriella the deed to the *fazenda* and she could have it. As for the rest...DNA tests. Blood tests. Sure, but who was he kidding? The child was his. The blue eyes. The dark hair. Besides, he knew Gabriella. She wouldn't lie to him. There wasn't a deceitful bone in her body.

Her lush, beautiful body— And what did that matter?

She was out of his life. That was what he'd wanted the night he broke up with her; it was what he wanted now. But he'd do the right thing. Give her the ranch. Set up a trust fund for the kid. Another for her. And that would be the end of it.

The absolute, complete end.

Then he'd get on with his life.

CHAPTER SEVEN

HE DIDN'T go to the *fazenda* or the hotel.

What would be the point?

He didn't need to see Gabriella and he certainly didn't need a room. His stay in Bonito would be brief, a couple of hours at most. All he had to do was meet with de Souza, set things up, then turn around and head home.

He arranged for the pilot and plane to remain on call, phoned to arrange for another rental vehicle, then phoned the *advogado,* who sounded astonished to hear that he was in Bonito.

"I thought you had returned to New York, *Senhor* Orsini."

"You thought wrong. I wish to see you this morning, *senhor.*"

De Souza hesitated. "That is not much notice. Let me put you through to my secretary. She can check my appointment schedule—"

"I'll be at your office in half an hour," Dante said, and ended the call.

He grabbed a cup of coffee on his way to the car rental counter. His stomach growled as he sipped the hot liquid, reminding him that he hadn't eaten in a while. First things first. The meeting with the lawyer. Get the legal details out of the way. Then there'd be time for everything else.

For getting his life on track.

De Souza sprang to his feet when Dante stepped into his office. Did the *senhor* want anything to drink? Coffee? Water? It was early but perhaps a *capirihana?* Dante thanked him, said he wanted nothing and wondered at the drops of sweat on the lawyer's shiny brow. It was a hot day but not in here; if anything, the AC was set to an uncomfortable low. When he shook de Souza's extended hand, it was like shaking hands with a chunk of ice.

The man was nervous, but why?

"Sit down, please, *Senhor* Orsini. This is an unexpected pleasure, but I am afraid my time is limited. Had you called last evening—"

"My time is limited, as well," Dante said briskly. He took the chair in front of the lawyer's desk and opened the black leather briefcase he'd brought with him. "So let's get straight to business. I want the deed to Viera y Filho transferred to *Senhorita* Reyes immediately. What will you require from me?"

The attorney took a pristine white handkerchief from his breast pocket and delicately mopped his brow.

"A transfer," he said. "But when you left without making those arrangements, I assumed—"

"I signed some papers after the auction yesterday." Dante took the papers from the briefcase and slid them across the desk. "They're in Portuguese, of course, but I've seen enough such documents to assume the blank lines on the last page are where I'd sign to transfer ownership."

De Souza barely glanced at the papers.

"Actually…actually, it's a bit more complicated than

that, *senhor.* The documents you signed should have been accompanied by a check."

"They were accompanied by a check." The *advogado* was shaking his head. Dante frowned. "What?"

"The check must be a—what do you call it? A check authorized by a bank."

"A cashier's check? I understand that, but I didn't have one with me. I had no way of knowing the auction was taking place yesterday morning and I definitely had no idea how much I would bid, but the auctioneer said— Dammit, de Souza, why do you keep shaking your head? Is there a problem? Fine. I'll call my bank. They can wire the funds here, to you or to the bank, or—" Dante narrowed his eyes until they were an icy blue glimmer. "Now what?"

"Twenty-four hours have passed, *Senhor* Orsini." De Souza gave an expressive shrug. "You have forfeited your option to the property."

"That's ridiculous!"

"It is in the contract you signed."

"Well, what happens now? Do I contact the auctioneer? The bank? Surely we don't have to go through that bidding process all over again?"

"There will be no bidding process, *senhor.*"

"Well, that's something." Dante took his cell phone from his pocket. "I'll contact my bank in New York while you contact the bank—"

"The property has already been purchased."

Dante felt his body stiffen. He had participated in enough tough business deals to sense that the statement was not a negotiating tactic.

"Purchased," he said softly.

"*Sim.*"

"By whom?" Dante asked, though he was sure he knew the answer.

De Souza looked at him and flushed.

"Understand, please, I am simply the legal tool of the bank in the transaction."

Dante rose slowly from the chair. "Answer the question. Who bought it?"

The lawyer swallowed hard. "*Senhor* Ferrantes."

Dante wanted to haul de Souza to his feet.

"You were supposed to be working for Gabriella," he growled, "but you were working for Ferrantes all along."

"You must understand. *Senhor* Ferrantes is an important member of our community."

Dante reached across the desk, took some small satisfaction as the lawyer shrank back in his chair. He scooped up the documents, stuffed them into the briefcase and stalked out the door. Out in the street again, he drew a deep breath as he took out his cell phone and called his own attorney. Sam was a senior partner at one of New York's most respected law firms; Dante used his private number and Sam answered on the second ring.

"Dante," he said pleasantly, "good to hear from—"

"Sam. I have a problem."

"Tell me," Sam said.

Dante gave him all the details. Well, almost all. He didn't mention that he'd had a prior relationship with Gabriella Reyes. He damned well didn't say that there was a strong possibility he had a son. What he explained, in concise terms, was that he was in Brazil, that he'd bid on a property and paid for it with a check that been deemed unacceptable twenty-four hours after the fact, and that the property in question had now been sold to someone else.

But he and his lawyer had gone to school together. Sam knew him well. Too well. There was a silence after Dante finished talking. Then Sam cleared his throat.

"What else?" he said. "Come on, man. I know there's

more to this than you're saying. You want me to give you an opinion that has teeth, I need to hear the rest."

So Dante told him. About Gabriella. That he and she had once been—that they had been involved. That she had a child. That it was his.

"You mean," Sam said coolly, "she says it's yours."

A muscled knotted in Dante's jaw. "Yes."

"And you want to believe her."

"Yes. No. Dammit, she's not a liar—"

Sam interrupted. Asked him if the word *option* had ever been mentioned in the sale of the ranch, asked him for the name and phone number of the bank that had foreclosed on it, then said he'd get back to him in ten minutes.

The line went dead.

Dante stood in the heat of the Brazilian sun, impatience and anger humming through him. He wanted to go back into de Souza's office, drag the man to his feet and show him what happened to those who sold out to the devil. Better still, he wanted to find Ferrantes and beat the crap out of him.

Logic prevailed.

He was in a strange country. His best bet was to let his lawyer find the appropriate legal solution, which he was doing right now. Ten minutes wasn't that long to wait.

There was a café next door. He went inside, ordered coffee, sat at a small table and drank the coffee while he waited, eyes glued to his watch. Was the damned thing working? The minute hand seemed not to move. And then his phone rang and he flipped it open.

"Dante," Sam said.

"Well?"

"The easy stuff first. Don't make any legal commitments to the woman. Be pleasant, stay calm, but—I hate to use the word—keep your options open until we do some tests. Okay?"

It was solid legal advice. "Okay. What about the property issue?"

"The property." Sam exhaled noisily. "You want it in legalese or words of one syllable?"

A muscle flexed in Dante's jaw. It didn't take a genius to know that Sam had not asked him a question meant to raise his hopes.

"Just tell me the bottom line."

"The bottom line, dude, is that you're screwed."

"Screwed how? You mean, the bidding process has to begin all over again?"

"I mean," Sam said carefully, "you bought an option to purchase the property and the option expired twenty-four hours from the moment you signed it. In other words, you have no further legal rights to it."

Dante sprang to his feet. The other customers in the café shot him wary looks. He ignored them, tossed his coffee cup in the trash and stormed outside.

"I made the winning bid," he said sharply. "The bank accepted it."

"The auctioneer accepted it."

"As the bank's rightful agent. Listen here, Sam—"

"The guy who bought the property after the twenty-four hours were up is a national."

"The twenty-four-hour thing is bull!"

"Maybe. But you're not on a level playing field, Dante. You're not in the U.S. of A., you're in another country. Is what they've done legal?" Sam Cohen's lift of the shoulders all but came through the phone. "Probably, but who knows? The only certainty is that you'd need a Brazilian attorney to walk you through this. I can get a name, fly down, meet with you and whatever guy is recommended, but—"

"There's no time for all that," Dante said grimly.

"Yeah. I figured as much. And, to be blunt, I can't guarantee how it would work out. My best advice? Find yourself another ranch, man. Hey, you're in Brazil. How tough could that be?"

Dante laughed. Even to his own ears, it was not a happy sound. He thanked his lawyer, disconnected and headed for his car.

Somehow the *fazenda* looked worse today than yesterday.

The potholes in the road seemed more numerous, the weeds higher, the house and outbuildings more forlorn. Dante parked, walked up the steps to the door and rang the bell. He could hear it echoing through the rooms.

He rang it again. And again. Finally the door swung open. A white-haired woman in a shapeless flowered dress scowled at him. She barked a question he figured was either what do you want or who are you? So he told her his name and said he wanted to see *Senhorita* Reyes.

The woman stood immobile. He started to repeat what he'd said when he heard Gabriella's voice. He brushed past the woman, who hurried after him, and followed the sound to what seemed to be a library although, like everything else here, it had seen better times.

Gabriella's back was to him as she squatted beside a cardboard box half-filled with books. She wore jeans and a T-shirt; the shirt had ridden up and he could see the ridge of her spine. Her hair was pulled back and secured with one of those things that looked like a rubber band but wasn't. Her feet were bare and dusty.

She was, in other words, a mess.

And she was beautiful. So beautiful, she made his heart ache.

"Yara," she said, without looking around, "*quem está aí?* Is it the man with the truck? If it is—"

"Hello, Gabriella."

Gabriella sprang to her feet so quickly that she kicked over a stack of books piled on the floor. That voice. She had never expected to hear it again. Never wanted to hear it again—and yet, the sound of it made her heartbeat quicken. And when she turned and saw Dante, the joy that swept through her was indescribable.

The intensity of it shocked her. Joy? For what? This man meant nothing to her. She meant nothing to him. She put her hand to her temple, where last night's headache had taken up what felt like permanent residence.

She was coming down with something, and was that not perfect timing?

This was even worse timing. That Dante should turn up again…

And why was he looking at her that way? As if she were a…a specimen in a zoo. She was a mess; she knew it. She'd dressed for the work of the day. A torn shirt. Ragged jeans. In New York, she had dressed for him, she had done everything for him because she had been fool enough to think she mattered to him.

But she never had.

She'd just been another of the endless string of shadow women who moved through his life, and if she'd lasted a little longer than most, so what? It had all come to nothing in the end.

Dante had never known the real her.

But she knew the real Dante Orsini. The man who had it all, who never looked back, who believed commitment to a relationship didn't involve anything deeper than temporary exclusivity and pricey gifts, although there had been times like that one weekend, that lovely, glorious weekend…

"What are you doing?"

He was looking from her to the box of dusty books, scowling as if he'd discovered something unpleasant on his shoe. It made her angry. Everything about him made her angry, especially after last night. To think she'd been fool enough to believe he'd really wanted to help her…

She blew an errant curl off her forehead.

"I have a better question," she said coldly. "What are *you* doing here?"

He flashed a quick smile. "Such a warm greeting."

Gabriella narrowed her eyes. "My lawyer told me you went back to New York."

"Your lawyer," he said, his mouth twisting. "Is that what you think that double-dealing bastard is?"

"Answer my question. Why didn't you return to the States?"

"I started to." He moved slowly toward her. "But I thought things over and I realized…I decided to come back and try to sort things out."

"There's nothing to sort out. Not anymore." Her chin rose. "*Senhor* de Souza explained everything to me. You chose not to buy the *fazenda* after all, and Ferrantes—"

"De Souza's a liar!"

"Is he?" Her chin rose. "Then why is Ferrantes the new owner of Viera y Filho?"

"He's the new owner because your wonderful attorney sold you out! He and Ferrantes and the bank sneaked a joker into the deck. I didn't know a damned thing about it until I saw de Souza an hour ago."

She gave a weary shrug. "It does not matter. You had already decided not to give the ranch to me. You made that clear. And that was for the best. It was a mistake for me to have asked such a thing of you."

"It wasn't a mistake, dammit! You had every right to ask. You and I were—we were close, once."

"No," she said stiffly, "we were not close. We were a man and a woman who came together in bed. Nothing more."

She was right. That was how it had been, how he had wanted it. Then why did hearing those words make him so angry? Like it or not, there'd been more between them than sex. Like the weekend they'd gone away to his house in Connecticut, the one Nick had dragged him north to look at and he'd ended up buying instead of Nick. He'd planned two long days and nights of making love, but the house hadn't cooperated. It had been built in the 1600s, and that weekend every piece of it decided to admit its age. You turned a faucet, the indoor plumbing—installed in the 1800s—coughed once and that was it. You turned on the furnace, vintage early 1900s, and nothing happened. The refrigerator—a handsome 1950s antique—groaned and died. And then there was the final insult: a storm sprang up and rain found a hole in the roof, right over their bed.

So, no. There had not been two days and nights of endless sex…but they'd had a wonderful time, anyway.

He'd turned up an old Scrabble set and she'd beaten him, three games running. She'd beaten him at gin, too, and at checkers, and he'd sighed and hung his head and talked her into one more game of everything, Scrabble and gin and checkers, winner take all, and when he won each and every time, she accused him of letting her win the first time around and he grinned, pulled her into his arms and said the "all" he wanted was her, naked in front of the fire-place….

Dammit, what did old memories have to do with

anything? He'd come here to do exactly what he'd said. To sort things out, nothing more.

"There's no sense debating our relationship," he said gruffly.

"I agree. So if that is what you came here to do—"

"It isn't. I was on my way home and then I began to think about things."

"What things?"

Dante looked at the woman who'd let him into the house. She stood, arms folded over her ample bosom, glaring at him as if he were here to steal the family silver.

"Do me a favor, okay? Ask your guard dog to step out of the room."

Gabriella laughed. Yara, a native of the Pantanal, *did* look as if she was standing guard. She'd stood that same way early this morning, when Ferrantes had come by, unannounced, with his ugly news.

Dante, for all his faults, was not Andre. He had hurt her heart once, he had even managed to hurt it again yesterday, but he would never hurt her physically.

She told that to Yara. "You can leave us alone," she said, in a rapid burst of Portuguese. "This man will not hurt me."

Yara's bushy eyebrows drew together. "What you mean is that he will not strike you."

Gabriella smiled at the old woman's wisdom.

"No. He will not."

"But he will hurt you in other ways."

Gabriella shook her head. "He no longer has that kind of power over me."

Yara made a sound that made it clear she did not believe that. Still, she threw Dante one last meaningful look and left the room. Gabriella wiped her dusty hands on her jeans and looked at Dante.

"Now," she said, "tell me why you have come here."

Dante took a deep breath. Where to start? He thought of all the tough business meetings he'd survived, of how there was always the right thing to say and the right way to say it, knew that this was going to be more difficult than any of those, and that the only way to handle it was head-on.

"I came back because of the boy. Daniel."

Gabriella raised an eyebrow. "This time he has a name?"

"To tell you that…that I accept responsibility for him."

"He has a name—and you've had a change in attitude. How interesting."

"Dammit, you're not making this easy…"

"Did you expect that I would? Get to the point, please. I have much to do."

Dante took another deep breath. "I had time to think. And I realized that I want to do the right thing for him. For you both. If he's my son—"

"If?" she said coldly. "*If* he is your son?"

"Gabriella, you know what I mean."

"No. I do not. Why don't you explain it to me?"

"Try looking at this from my vantage point. You walked out. I didn't hear a word from you, and all of a sudden here's this child—"

She moved quickly, covering the distance between them before he could think, and lifted her furious face to his.

"You keep saying that I walked out. I did not. *You* did the walking, *senhor*. And no, you did not hear a word from me. Why would you? What could we have said that had not already been said by you that night you sent me away?"

"All right." His mouth thinned. "Have it your way. This has to do with the baby. With Daniel. If he's mine—"

"Stop saying that! Do you think I would lie about such a thing? That I would have slept with another man after—"

"Would you?" Dante's voice was rough. "Would you

have slept with another man after you'd been with me?" He moved forward quickly, framed her face with his hands, forced her to look up at him. "Because I don't want to think of you that way, Gabriella, I don't want to think of you in someone else's bed with your hands on him the way they used to be on me, your mouth on his, your skin hot against his."

"Damn you, Dante," she said in a shaky whisper, "damn you, damn you, damn—"

He kissed her.

Kissed her hard, with anger, forcing her lips to part to the thrust of his tongue, and when she cried out against his mouth he groaned, his kiss gentled and he gathered her against him, ignoring the way her hands rose to flatten against his chest and push him away. He kept kissing her, slanting his mouth over hers again and again as if he would consume her sweet taste, and at last she gave that little moan of surrender he had always loved, rose to him, wound her arms around his neck and kissed him back.

But her acquiescence didn't last. A heartbeat later she tore her mouth from his.

"Please. If you ever cared for me, let me go."

He didn't want to. He wanted to hold her forever, which was crazy. He was here for the child, not for any other reason. So he took a steadying breath, dropped his hands to his sides and stepped back.

"Tell me about Ferrantes."

Her eyes flashed.

"No," he said quickly, "I don't mean— Tell me what's happening. De Souza says he's bought this place. Has he contacted you?"

Gabriella shivered and wrapped her arms around herself.

"*Sim.* He was here this morning." She touched the tip

of her tongue to her lips. "He gave me—he gave me an…
an— I do not know what you call it. A decision I must
make."

"An ultimatum?"

"Yes. Either he gets what he wants," she said, so softly
Dante had to bend his head to hear her, "or he will sell Viera
y Filho to the rancher who owns the adjoining 50,000
hectares."

Dante nodded. "And what he wants," he said tonelessly,
"is you."

She looked up, eyes bright with determination. "I told
him what he could do with his ultimatum. And he told
me—"

"He told you…?"

She shrugged, turned away, began taking books from
the shelves. "He said it was my choice, that I could do as
he demanded or I had until this evening to leave this
place."

A string of Sicilian profanities, learned on the streets
of his childhood, fell from Dante's lips. "He can't do
that."

Gabriella swung toward him. "Of course he can!"

She was right. Ferrantes could do any damned thing he
wanted, or so it seemed.

"But where will you go?"

Another shrug, her face once more averted. "Yara can
take us in for a few weeks."

"Yara. The guard dog?"

"She is a good woman. She all but raised me."

"She has a house you can share?"

Gabriella thought of Yara's house. Small. Very small.
Smaller still, these last months since Yara's daughter, son-
in-law and their three small children had come to live with
her and her husband.

"Yes."

It was the least certain "yes" Dante had ever heard. He stepped in front of Gabriella, took a book from her hands, set it aside and clasped her shoulders.

"To hell with that."

Her eyes, filled with defiance, met his.

"I will do what I must."

"There's no room at Yara's for you and the baby," he said flatly, "is there?"

"I will do what I must," she said again.

He nodded. She would. She had done what she had to do all these months, returning to Brazil to have her child, living out here in the middle of nowhere with nothing but the barren land for company.

"Is your clothing packed?"

Her eyebrows rose. "Why?"

"Dammit, just answer the question. I can hire someone to pack this stuff, whatever you don't want to leave behind."

"I am perfectly capable of doing it myself."

He took a deep breath. "I'm taking you with me. To New York."

She stared at him as if he'd lost his sanity. "Why would you do that? Why would I *permit* you to do that?"

"Because I say so."

She looked up into his eyes. He meant every word; she knew it. The blood of his ancestors flowed within him. He was a man who would not tolerate any obstacles once he had decided he wanted something.

There had been times he'd been like that in bed.

The tender Dante, the sweet lover she'd adored, would vanish. His lovemaking would turn hot and hungry. He'd clasp her wrists, hold her arms above her head, say things, tell her things while he was deep inside her, while his body moved within hers, and at those moments she would come and come and come…

"I do not take orders from you," she said, forcing the unwelcome memories away.

A muscle knotted in his jaw. "Listen to me, I can't leave you here alone, and I can't stay with you. You must come with me. You and the baby."

"The baby." Her voice broke. "The baby you still think does not belong to you."

He knew what she wanted him to say, but he couldn't bring himself to say it. "There's no other solution."

She shook her head. "It is all happening too fast," she whispered. "Much, much too fast. I need time to think. To plan."

She was right about everything happening fast. He'd come back to Brazil to make careful arrangements. Give her the *fazenda*, arrange for paternity tests, set up funds for her and the child, do all the right things but do them logically and slowly.

Taking her with him flew in the face of all that.

His plan had turned into no plan at all, certainly not one Sam or any other good attorney would advise, much less approve.

And yet, what else could he do? Leave her to the not so tender mercies of Ferrantes?

"It *is* quick," he said, because what good would it be to lie? He framed her face with his hands and slowly raised it to his. "We'll work out the details later. And it will all work out. You'll see."

She hesitated. He could almost see her weighing his words.

"Dante," she said, "I do not think—"

"Good," he said softly. "Don't think. Just trust me. Say you'll come with me."

She wanted to trust him. At least, her heart did. Her head said something else…but then he bent to her and kissed her and, like a fool, she agreed.

CHAPTER EIGHT

DANTE stood on the wraparound terrace of his two-story Central Park West penthouse, a cup of rapidly cooling coffee in his hand.

Was it possible he'd been away from New York for only two days?

It felt more like weeks.

Either autumn had suddenly overtaken the park or he simply hadn't noticed it, now that the leaves of the maples, oaks and sycamores far below were turning rich shades of crimson, brown and gold. Up here the mums and asters and who-knew-what-else his sister Isabella had planted in big redwood tubs had burst into vivid bloom.

Izzy would be thrilled.

She'd planted them last spring. Even when she was a kid, she'd loved to dig around in the dirt. Cesare would spend hours in the fenced-in yard behind the house in the Village, planting, then feeding and watering his annual crop of tomatoes. Izzy would accompany him, down on all fours tending the scraggly daisies that seemed the only flowers hardy enough to survive the Manhattan air. Now, all grown up, she'd taken one look at Dante's terrace after he'd bought the penthouse, gotten a dreamy look and said she could just imagine how perfect some plantings would be here, and here, and here....

So he'd let her poke and plant, he'd teased her like crazy and the result had been a summer of roses and daffs and other stuff, and now here came autumn.

His first reaction, seeing the blaze of color this morning, was to grab the phone, call her and say, "Hey, Iz, so maybe playing in the dirt isn't such a bad thing."

"It's called gardening, you idiot," Iz would say, and laugh.

Except, he couldn't tell her.

She'd want to come by, and how could he let that happen because if she did stop over, if any of his family did, how in hell would he explain the woman and baby living in the guest suite? Would he say, "Hi, good to see you and by the way, this is Gabriella—no, I don't think I ever introduced you to her before, Mama, and oh, by the way, this is her baby who might, emphasis on the 'might,' also be mine and yeah, that 'might' is important because somehow or other, I blew straight past the whole DNA/blood-test/paternity-test thing..."

Right. That would work out just fine. His mother would pass out, his sisters would shriek, his brothers would tell him he was an idiot, and his father would laugh and say that obviously, the trip to Brazil had not taught him anything about negotiating.

Dante took a long breath.

Maybe the problem was he'd come up against someone who was a hell of a lot better at negotiating than he'd ever been.

He raised the coffee cup and drank. Maybe caffeine would help. God knew, something had to. What in hell had he been thinking yesterday? Better still, had he really convinced Gabriella to come north…or had she played her role so well that she'd convinced him to ask her to do it?

At this point he honestly didn't know.

The only certainty was that yesterday's brilliant plan was clearly today's potential disaster. Either he'd been manipulated big-time or he'd lost his sanity. However he looked at it, the truth was that he didn't have any idea how he could have thought bringing her and the kid home with him would be a good idea.

How could it be?

The only positive thing was that nobody knew about this mess. And he had to keep it that way until it was resolved. Not easy, considering the presence of the woman and child sleeping in the guest suite, but if he moved fast, he could do it. Nobody even knew he was back. His office didn't expect him for a couple more days. Neither did his brothers. He'd given his housekeeper a few days off because he hadn't known exactly how long he'd be gone; he'd told his driver the same thing. The night doorman had been on duty, ditto the concierge, but why would anybody question them?

At least he had some breathing room.

As for why he'd acted so foolishly…he had no ready answer. Maybe he'd been punchy from lack of sleep. From all the flying back and forth. From the shock of seeing Gabriella again. From looking at a baby and being told it was his.

Dante slugged down more of the coffee and shuddered. It was cold, oily and acrid but he drank it with grim determination. He'd brewed the pot hours ago, knowing he needed the jolt, trying to come up with a plan. Gabriella, thanks for small favors, was still sleeping. She and the baby. At least, he assumed they were because there hadn't been a sound from the guest suite. He'd taken her there as soon as they'd stepped from his private elevator and there hadn't been a whisper from it since.

Not that they'd exchanged so much as a word during the flight home.

"There's a small room in the rear of the plane, *senhor*," the attendant had told him in hushed terms when she saw Gabriella board with a swaddled infant in her arms. "The lady might find it more comfortable."

That was where Gabriella had spent the entire flight, curled up on a sofa in that room, the kid asleep in a contraption that looked more like the kind of pack frame he'd used hiking in Alaska than a thing meant for carrying a kid but, hey, what did he know about babies?

Nada, he thought grimly, *niente,* zip. He didn't have one fact in his head about babies beyond that they were small. And that was how he'd always liked it. He'd never been one of those guys who got off thinking about someday having children. Truth was, he always had to fake it when somebody showed him baby pictures. You had to say something, he understood that, and his standard response was "Cute," accompanied by a big smile, the same as he'd done that day in the lobby.

Was it his fault children, especially babies, looked pretty much alike? Or that they didn't much interest him at this point in his life? Someday, maybe, but surely not yet.

Which led to the distinct possibility that he might have moved too quickly in this entire situation, and yes, that was absolutely the word for it even though he knew better than to use it again with Gabriella.

Simply put, he'd made an enormous mistake.

The plan he'd started with—sitting down with Sam Cohen, arranging for paternity tests and, if they panned out, establishing the necessary trust funds—had been the right one. So what if the bank had sold Viera y Filho to

Ferrantes? A ranch, as Sam had so reasonably pointed out, was just a ranch. He could have found another place for Gabriella, left her there while he flew home and arranged all the rest. She'd have been safe from Ferrantes, safe from poverty…

And five thousand miles from him.

A muscle knotted in his jaw.

A little distance between them would have had nothing to do with his Doing The Right Thing. There was no reason for her to be here where he could see her face. Smell the unique delicacy of her perfume. Know that she'd spent the night just down the hall from his bedroom…

"Dammit," he muttered, and strode from the terrace into the living room.

That was precisely the kind of crap that had brought him to this point. How could a man cling to reason when a woman who had once shared his bed sighed as he kissed her? How could he think straight when she returned his kisses as if she'd been aching for them? That had always been one of the things that had gotten to him about her, the way she'd made him feel as if he was the only man who'd ever mattered. That he was important to her.

That she'd been becoming important to him.

Dante snorted as he dumped the rest of the coffee into the kitchen sink.

Why think about all this stuff again, especially since it was ridiculous? She was beautiful and bright; they'd had fun together and she was amazing in bed. End of story.

That she could still affect him, still push the right buttons, was not good. Dante narrowed his eyes.

Responding to his kisses even as she faced him with apparent defiance, holding herself aloof even as she trembled in his arms, insisting she wanted nothing from him after saying her son was his…

Just look where that had landed him.

He'd left here a couple of days ago to deal with a problem of his father's. Instead, he'd found himself facing a problem of his own—a potentially life-changing problem he had to confront head-on. He dealt with problems every day of his life. It was how he'd helped make Orsini's into a world-class investment firm that remained respected and rock solid even in the current economic nightmare.

He'd aced Financial Analysis 101. So, how come he'd made such a muck-up of Real-Life Analysis, Grade School Level?

It was time to start making some intelligent moves, starting with settling Gabriella and the kid elsewhere. The real estate agent who'd got him this place understood his tastes, his needs; the guy's firm was a high-end operation that understood the importance of discretion. That would be step one. Find her a place to live. Someplace within hailing distance but not where anyone would stumble over her.

He thought about that for a moment. To someone not familiar with the circumstances, a set-up like that would look as if he were trying to deny the ramifications of the situation.

Ridiculous.

He was just doing what he should have done in the first place. Behaving intelligently. Sam Cohen would surely agree. Not that he'd involve him until he had the move in motion, otherwise he'd have to admit Sam had an ass for a client.

Dante smiled thinly. He'd call Sam later today, set up an appointment, arrange for the necessary tests, for temporary financial support, long-term if that proved necessary because hadn't he finally faced the fact that anything was possible?

For no discernible reason, an image of Gabriella flashed before him.

Her wide eyes. Her lovely mouth. Her smile. And, though it wasn't something one could see, her honesty all the time they'd been together, starting the first time he'd phoned.

"It's Dante Orsini," he'd said, and then, because the need to see her had been near all consuming, he'd skipped the niceties and gone straight to the point. "I'll be there at eight, to take you to dinner."

"Did I miss something?" she'd said, with a little laugh. "When, exactly, did you ask me out?"

"I didn't," he'd replied bluntly. "Why would I ask you for something we both want?"

He'd heard the catch of her breath. And then she'd said, "Yes." Just that one word, that "yes," delivered in such a low, sexy voice that it had filled him with heat.

She was into honesty from the small things to the big ones. She'd told him she was a Jets fan when he said he was into the Giants. He'd mentioned his preference for the Giants to an endless stream of women and every last one had quickly said wasn't that nice because she loved them, too, and that included the ones who probably couldn't tell a football from a volley ball.

She ate with gusto, packing away a loaded-with-everything hot dog at a Yankees game, warning him she knew no bounds when it came to lobster and proving it by finishing every bite at The Boathouse, ending with butter on her chin that he'd just had to kiss away.

She was upfront about everything.

Especially in bed.

Her passion, her arousal, her eagerness when he touched her, when he tasted her breasts, when he put his mouth on that perfect bud between her thighs, all of it so real, so sweet, so amazing it shook his world.

And when she responded, when she caressed him, put her hands and mouth on him...

"Dammit," he growled.

None of that meant he should believe this child was his without proof, he thought coldly.

First things first. Shower. Phone that real estate agent. And then tap politely at Gabriella's door, tell her he'd been thinking things over and that he'd come up with a workable plan.

He felt better already.

Showered, shaved, dressed in faded jeans and a navy T-shirt, Dante headed for the kitchen.

He'd lost track not only of days but of hours. All that going back and forth had confused his internal clock. Was it time for breakfast? Lunch? Dinner? He didn't know and didn't much care. He was hungry, was all he knew; his stomach was growling. He'd had a sandwich on the plane but that seemed a long time ago. Gabriella hadn't eaten at all. During the flight, the attendant had said she'd checked and both Gabriella and the baby were sleeping. He'd thought about going back there, just to see how things were, but if Gabriella was asleep...

Okay. So maybe the truth was, he hadn't been ready to talk to her. Not then.

But he was ready now.

So, he'd cook something for the two of them.

He frowned as he opened the fridge. The shelves were pretty empty except for the requisite things. Eggs. Bread. Butter. A container of light cream that passed the sniff test. An unopened quart of milk. There was a wedge of cheddar in the cheese keeper on the door. He wasn't the world's best cook but he could put together a cheese omelet, make some toast, a pot of coffee. As for the baby...

What did babies that small eat? Formula? Little jars of vile-looking, strange-colored food? Not that it would be his problem. Gabriella had filled a big carry-on with what she'd called baby stuff. She surely had food for the kid inside it.

He took out the eggs, the milk, the butter, the cheese—

And hesitated.

Come to think of it, how come it was so quiet? He'd been up and pacing around for hours. He figured Gabriella was exhausted, but still, what about the kid? When his sister Anna was a baby, she'd cried nonstop.

For no good reason the skin on the back of his neck prickled. He shut the refrigerator door and headed up the stairs.

Nothing. No sounds at all drifting down the wide hall.

He paused at the guest suite. "Gabriella?" He moved closer to the door. Tapped at it. "Gabriella?" No answer. "Gabriella," he said loudly, and then he said to hell with it, turned the knob and stepped inside.

The curtains in the sitting room were drawn. Beyond, the bedroom door stood open. He walked toward it.

The baby lay on the bed, surrounded by pillows. He was on his belly, his rump up in the air, head to the side and part of his fist jammed into his mouth. He was sound asleep and... Dante frowned. Hell. The kid was that all-purpose word. Cute. A cliché but accurate. The kid was so small, the bed so big...

Dante cleared his throat. He hadn't come up here to look at babies, he'd come to check on Gabriella. Obviously, she was in the bathroom.

Oh, hell.

The bathroom door was shut but the sound of someone

being sick traveled straight through it. "Gabriella?" he said, hurrying to the door. "Are you sick?"

"Dante." Her voice was weak. Frighteningly weak. "Don't come in. I have a bug. The flu—"

He could almost feel the blood draining from his face. He wasn't good at this, either. Somebody throwing up...

Gabriella groaned. Retched. He didn't think, didn't hesitate; he flung the door open and stepped into the room. His Gabriella was hunched over the toilet, her hair streaming down her back, her body trembling. He cursed, ran to her and clasped her shoulders from behind.

"Sweetheart. Why didn't you ask me to help you? I'll get a doctor—"

"Go away. I don't need—"

She retched again. His hands tightened on her. He could feel her shaking; she was wearing a nightgown and she was soaked straight through with sweat. His heart turned over.

"Gaby. Honey, what can I do to help?"

What could he do? If she hadn't felt as if she were dying, Gabriella would have laughed. What he could do was disappear. This was not what a woman wanted, to have a man see her like this. Sweaty, disheveled—and throwing up everything, starting at her toes.

Pain fisted in her belly and she bent over and gave herself up to the spasm. By the time it ended, she was swaying on her feet. Dante cursed softly, drew her gently back against him. *Go away,* she thought desperately, *just go away.*

But his body felt so good against hers. Strong. Hard. Comforting. Shivering, icy cold, she let his warmth seep into her.

"Gaby?"

His voice was filled with alarm. She wanted to reassure

him that she'd be okay, that she'd come down with whatever had sickened Yara the week before, but it happened again, the wave of agonizing nausea, and she gagged, leaned forward and vomited.

When she straightened up this time, she knew the spasms were over.

"I'm okay now," she said weakly.

She reached out to flush the toilet but Dante did it instead. She felt her face fill with heat. *Deus,* the embarrassment of it! That he should see her like this, desperate and all but helpless when she prided herself on her independence, when it was, she knew, one of the things that had drawn him to her.

Not that she cared about that anymore; it didn't matter if he was drawn to her or not. Still, it was—it was—

"Here," he said gently.

He brought a cup of water to her lips. She wanted to tell him she didn't need his help, but that would have been a lie. Instead, she sipped the cool liquid, rinsed her mouth, spat it out. She did it twice and then he eased her onto the closed toilet and washed her face with a soft, damp washcloth.

"Better?"

She nodded. "Yes. Thank you. But really, you can go now. I'll be—"

"Do not," he said quietly, "tell me what I can do, Gabriella." He bent, lifted her in his arms and carried her into the bedroom. "I know exactly what I can do. What I'm going to do. And it starts with putting you to bed and calling the doctor, whether you like it or not."

"No. I do not need—"

She followed his gaze to the bed, sighing with relief when she saw that Daniel had slept through it all.

Dante headed for the door.

"Where are you taking me?"

"Don't worry. I'll come back for the baby after I get you settled."

"But—"

Arguing was pointless. She knew that. Once Dante made up his mind to do something, nothing would deter him. She had no choice but to loop her arms around his neck and give in as he carried her down the corridor. When he shouldered open a door and she saw that he had brought her to his bedroom, sick as she was it sent a little thrill of recognition through her. She had not been here in a very, very long time but it looked the same. Big, masculine. A perfect reflection of the man who had once been her lover.

He carried her to the bed. His bed. As he eased her back against the pillows, she thought of how many times he had done that in the months they'd been together.

"Dante. Wait…"

Too late. He was gone, returning seconds later with Daniel in his arms. Her heart skipped a beat. Her son, in his father's powerful arms. The sight made her throat tighten. He gave Daniel to her while he arranged a pair of big, upholstered chairs so they faced each other, their soft, high arms forming the walls of an improvised crib. Then he took the still-sleeping baby from her, laid him gently in the improvised crib and covered him with a cashmere throw.

"Okay?" he said softly, looking at her.

Gabriella smiled. "Perfect. Thank you."

He nodded. His gaze swept over her; his dark eyebrows drew together. "You're soaked."

She looked down at herself. Her cotton nightgown, plastered to her skin with sweat, She flushed, slipped under the duvet and drew it to her chin. The bed smelled of Dante:

masculine, clean…wonderful. She looked up, ready to tell him she couldn't stay here but he was gone again. Of course. She felt her color deepen. He had done all she could possibly expect and more, held her while she was violently ill, taken care of the baby…

"Sit up."

She raised her head in surprise. His voice was gentle; he had a bowl of water, a towel and one of his T-shirts in his hands.

"Dante. Really—"

"Gabriella," he said softly, "really. Just relax, sweetheart, and let me take care of you."

No, she thought, no, she could not do that. Not even for these precious moments. She could not permit herself to fall under his spell again; it would break her, if she did. He was kind, he was generous, he was the most gorgeous man she had ever known, but there could never be more to it than that.

The cloth stroked lightly over her face. It felt wonderful. His nearness to her felt wonderful. Sighing, she closed her eyes and gave in. Let him bathe her face, her throat. Let him push aside the straps of her damp nightgown, run the warm cloth lightly over her shoulders, her arms…

The upper slope of her breasts.

His hand slowed. His breath quickened. So did hers. Her eyes flew open. Her lover's face was all harsh planes and angles, his pale-blue eyes blazed with flame.

"Gaby," he said hoarsely.

He had never called her that until today. There was something incredibly intimate in it. And when his hand paused, cupped her breast, she cried out at the pleasure of his touch. She was going to die from this. From wanting him. Needing him. Aching for him.

He said her name again, brushed his thumb across her

nipple, erect under the nightgown. He bent toward her, closer and closer—

A thin wail broke the silence. It was Daniel. Her son's cry grew stronger.

"The baby," she whispered.

Dante drew back. His hand fell away from her; he was all business now.

"Lift your arms," he said briskly, and when she did, he pulled the nightgown over her head, his gaze never dropping below her arms and face, and replaced the gown with the T-shirt. By the time she'd finished easing it down her body under cover of the duvet, he was leaning over her with the baby in his arms.

She reached for her son. Daniel was kicking and crying as if he had not nursed at her breasts only three hours ago. She smiled at her little boy, tugged down the loose neckline of the T-shirt and brought him to her breast. She did it without thinking; she had nursed him from the day of his birth, completely unselfconsciously…

But not in front of the man who had given her baby to her.

Dante made a soft sound. A groan. She looked up. His gaze was fixed on the baby, on his small hand against her breast, his small mouth at her nipple. A sensation so powerful it made her tremble swept through her. She whispered Dante's name. His eyes met hers; he groaned again, bent to her, cupped her face and took her mouth in a hot, hungry kiss.

And then he was gone.

CHAPTER NINE

THE baby nursed until Gabriella was certain she could almost feel his little tummy rounding under her hand. She shifted him to her shoulder, gently patted his back and was rewarded with a contented burp.

"That's my boy," she said softly. He gave her a happy grin and she laughed and played a round of I-See with him, forgetting everything for a few happy minutes. Her aching head and bones, her unsettled stomach...

Her unsettled life.

Daniel seemed to sense her change in mood. His dark, winged brows drew together. His sculpted lips turned down. His features were such a perfect duplication of Dante's...

Gabriella swallowed hard. "It's all right, *bebé*," she crooned. "Mama loves you. She'll always love you." She touched the tip of her finger to his nose. "We'll be fine, you and I. Just wait and see."

The baby's expression softened. He smiled. Yawned. Yawned again, and Gabriella scooted down in the big bed, holding him securely in the curve of her arm. In a few seconds he was fast asleep. The flight, the change in routine, had tired him.

She looked at the thick, dark lashes that lay against his

cheeks, noting again that he was the very image of his father. When her boy grew up, he and Dante would be mirror images.

Mirror images no one would see.

Dante had made it sound as if she and Daniel were to be part of his life, but she knew better. It wasn't that he'd lied but that he'd spoken under stress. He was, at heart, a decent man and he'd reacted with gallantry to her circumstances.

Reality had come after they'd boarded the plane. It had not been difficult to see. He had become distant. When the flight attendant suggested she and Daniel might be more comfortable in the small private room at the rear, Dante had said that was an excellent idea. It was, in a way. It had meant she could nurse the baby, change him, rock him to sleep in her arms without any distractions, but still...

Foolishly enough, she'd thought Dante might at least spend some time with her and the baby, but he had not entered the little room, not even once. It wasn't as if he'd forgotten their presence. He'd sent the attendant to her, several times.

Was everything all right? the woman had inquired politely. Did the *senhorita* need anything? If so, she had only to press the call button.

What Gabriella needed could not be gotten by pressing the call button. She hadn't said that, of course, she'd simply smiled politely and said she would be sure to do that. Then she'd fed the baby, put him into a fresh diaper, curled up on the sofa with him and fallen into a deep, dreamless sleep.

To her surprise, she'd slept for hours. She knew she was tired but it was as if only now, miles above the earth and from the *fazenda,* her mind and body were ready to admit she was not just tired but exhausted.

So much had happened during the past months! She had first tended to her father, then to her brother. Her father, true to form, had seemed to expect everything she'd done for him until his last breath; her brother, also true to form, had worried she was doing too much.

"You are with child," he'd said. "You must worry about a new life, Gabriella, not a worn-out one like mine."

Remembering those months before Arturo's death was bittersweet. They had been as close as when they'd been children—but all the while, she'd known she could not save him.

And she'd been pregnant. An easy pregnancy, thankfully, but still, she was exhausted all the time, going without sleep, worrying over the increasing awareness that her father had gambled away everything, that there was no money left in his accounts or, eventually, in hers. Looking back, it seemed as if she had done nothing but worry.

Then Dante had appeared.

For a little while, at least, she could lift her head, take a breath, make plans. Yes, he'd obviously realized what a burden he'd undertaken, but once she was in New York, things would be better. She'd lost the *fazenda* and that broke her heart, but perhaps the cold truth was that she'd be better off in Manhattan. She knew it better than she knew Bonito. She had friends in the city, contacts, her old agent. She could find a small apartment, get some modeling assignments, start to regain her feet.

She had thought about all those things during the flight, but by the time the plane landed she was sick. Whatever bug she'd been fighting had finally won. Everything ached; her belly felt as if someone had jabbed it with a hot poker.

She hid it from Dante. Not that he'd have abandoned her if he learned she was ill—she knew that. But the last thing she'd wanted was to be more of a burden than she already was. She would never have let him know she was sick if he hadn't stumbled across the information by accident.

But she would get better. She would not overstay her welcome. A few days. A week, at most, and she would move on.

She had to, she thought now, as the baby slept beside her. Oh, yes, she had to move on. And quickly, before her foolish heart led her into trouble. Into temptation. Look at what had happened a little while ago. That kiss. The whisper of Dante's fingers against her breast. She'd felt her body come alive, reminding her that she was not only a mother, she was a woman.

Yara had said she would be free of such urges for a very long time but clearly, her old *ama* was wrong. Those urges, those needs, were still there. They were there for Dante, only for Dante.

A light knock sounded at the closed door. Gabriella drew the duvet higher.

"Yes?"

"Is it okay to come in?"

It wasn't, not while her heart was pounding like this.

"*Sim.* Yes, of course."

Dante had a tray in his hands. There were things arranged on it. A carafe of iced water. A glass. A teapot, cup and saucer. A box of tissues. And a small brass bell.

"In case you're thirsty," he said briskly, making room on the teak night table. "And a bell, if you should need me."

"A bell," she said, as if she'd never heard the word before. Why wouldn't he look at her? Moments ago he had kissed her as if he would never get enough of kissing her and now…

"One of my sisters, Anna, brought it back from somewhere. Thailand. Katmandu. Wherever aging hippies go to die." He did look at her then, flashed a quick smile. "Not that Anna's an aging anything. I keep telling her she was born a few decades too late."

"Anna," Gabriella said, and it truly was a word she'd never heard before. In the months they'd been together, she'd met his brothers once, purely by chance, but Dante had never talked about his family. Of course, neither had she. "It's…it's a lovely name."

"Old-fashioned, Anna says, but…"

But what? Dante thought. Why was he talking about his sister? Was it because it was safer than doing what he really wanted to do, reaching for Gabriella, drawing her into his arms and kissing her until she wrapped her arms around his neck and begged him to finish what they had started a little while ago? No way. She was sick. He couldn't take advantage of her and besides, it would only complicate things—as if they weren't complicated enough.

He moved the pitcher of water, the glass, the teapot, did a handful of absolutely unnecessary things and then he stepped back.

"Okay," he said brightly. "As I said, if you need anything…"

"Thank you."

"Do you feel better?"

"I'm fine."

The hell she was. Her face was almost the same shade of ivory as the pillow. The baby, at least, looked okay. He was sleeping, lashes dusting his cheeks, mouth pursed in a small bow.

Cute.

Dante frowned. Wrong. The baby didn't look cute as much as he looked, well, like a miniature of a familiar face. A very familiar face…

He swallowed hard. Turned his gaze on Gabriella.

"Yeah. Well, we'll see what the doctor has to say."

"Dante. I don't need a—"

"Yes. You do."

"I don't. Honestly, Dante—"

"Honestly, Gabriella," he said, and then, because he damned well had to do it, he bent and kissed her, very lightly, on the mouth. "Ring the bell if you need me," he said, and then he was gone.

Gabriella glared at the closed door. Damn the man! Did he think he could give her orders? Kiss her into obedience? He had not changed at all. He still acted as if he owned the world.

She had hated that about him.

She had adored that about him.

Until he'd come into her life, she'd never known you could be furious at a man and crazy about him at the same time, but how could anyone hold Dante's macho arrogance against him? It was part of him and it was incredibly sexy. He'd shown it the first time he phoned to ask her out, except he hadn't "asked" her anything. He'd said hello, reminded her they'd met at a party a few nights before, and then he'd told her he'd be by at eight to take her to dinner.

"Did I miss something?" she'd said, even though she'd been hoping he would call. "I mean, exactly when did you ask me out?"

"Why should I ask you for something we both want?" he'd said in a low, husky voice.

Being sure of himself was part of who Dante Orsini was.

The trouble was, he was sure of her, too. Sure that she was mesmerized by him. And she had been. For all her air of cool sophistication, she'd been his from the start.

"I don't want you seeing anyone but me," he'd said, that very first night. She'd been in his arms by then. In his bed. In this bed. And he'd been deep, deep inside her. "You belong to me," he'd added, his voice rough. "You're mine. Do you understand that?"

Yes, she'd said, yes, yes, yes.

Gabriella blinked back the sudden threat of tears. Ridiculous. It had been fun. She had been faithful. So had Dante. He was, after all, a moral man. It was just that his interest in a woman never lasted all that long.

As for what seemed to be happening now…it meant nothing. He was a virile male in his prime. And she—she was a woman who had not had sex in quite a while.

All right.

She had not had sex since the night before he'd gone away on business.

The baby gave a little cry in his sleep. Gabriella drew him closer. She would get them out of here as fast as she could. A few phone calls would start the process. Then she'd thank Dante for all his help and say goodbye.

Another knock at the door.

Dante again. This time with a physician in tow. He introduced them, then left the room. If the doctor was surprised at finding a woman and an infant in Dante Orsini's bed, he gave no sign, simply examined her and then Daniel, who reacted to the insult to his small person with ear-splitting wails of protest.

The doctor packed away his stethoscope.

"You have a virus."

"I could have told you that," Gabriella said grumpily.

"The baby's fine," he said, ignoring her bad manners. "Has he ever had formula?"

"Yes, but why? Will it be dangerous for me to nurse him while I'm sick?"

"Not dangerous. Tiring. You need to rest. And to drink plenty of fluids. Let Mr. Orsini take care of things while you concentrate on getting better."

The doctor left. Dante reappeared. The ease with which he had taken over, making decisions for her, was, for some reason, infuriating. When he held out his hand and showed her the two capsules in his palm, she shook her head.

"No."

"No, what?"

"No, I'm not taking those things. Your doctor should know better than to prescribe antibiotics for a virus."

Dante rolled his eyes. "They're Tylenol."

Of course they were. And they'd help ease the ache in her bones, in her head. Another decision she'd let Dante make…and what did it matter? It was only temporary.

She took the capsules. Drank some water.

"More," Dante ordered.

She glowered at him but she finished what was in the glass.

"Thank you," Dante said, straight-faced. He took the glass, put it on the night table. Then he scooped the baby from the improvised crib where the doctor had put him.

"What are you doing?"

"Lie back. Close your eyes. Get some rest."

"Listen here, Dante, I am not yours to command. I am not a child—"

"Listen here, Gabriella," he said, spoiling it by flashing a grin that made her want to grin in return. She didn't, of course, and he swooped in to press a quick, soft kiss to her parted lips.

"You'll catch the flu," she said, because she had to say something or run the danger of kissing him back.

He touched the tip of his finger to her nose. "Time to take a nap."

"But Daniel…"

"Daniel and I will do just fine."

Hearing her son's name slip so softly and simply from

Dante's lips did something to her, something that left her knowing she dared not reply for danger of doing something stupid…like weeping. Instead she watched Dante stroll from the room, the baby pressed to his shoulder, her son's pale eyes filled with curiosity.

All right. She'd lie here for a few minutes. Then she'd go rescue the baby from a man who knew nothing about babies.

She awoke and knew that hours must have gone by.

Experimentally she stretched her limbs. She hurt a little but nowhere near as much as before.

Cautiously she sat up. Got to her feet. Her legs felt a little like undercooked pasta, but nothing major seemed wrong except that she needed to pee, desperately, and there wasn't a way in the world she was going to ring for Dante and ask him to help her with that.

She made it to the bathroom, sank down on the toilet, sighed with relief as she emptied her bladder. She flushed, gave the huge walk-in shower a longing glance but decided not to push her luck. Instead she washed her hands and face, used Dante's brush on her hair, automatically opened the drawer that had always held a couple of packaged toothbrushes, tried not to think of how many women had opened this same drawer in the past months, unwrapped a brush and cleaned her teeth.

She looked in the mirror.

Not great but it would have to do.

Dante's soft terry robe hung, as it always had, behind the door. She put it on over the T-shirt, paused in the bedroom to get a pair of panties and set out in search of her baby.

The enormous two-story penthouse was quiet. What

time was it? It was light outside, but barely. Was it night or was it day? Amazing, how she'd lost track of the hours.

She went down the wide, curved staircase, a cautious hand on the carved banister. Her legs had gone from feeling like undercooked spaghetti to spaghetti *al dente*. A good sign, surely…

Was that a sound? A voice? She paused at the foot of the stairs.

Yes. There was bright light at the end of the wide corridor she knew led to Dante's big, if rarely used, show-place of a kitchen. Slowly she made her way there, her bare feet soundless against the cool marble floor—and stopped at the entrance, eyes widening.

The voice she'd heard was Dante's. Barefoot the same as she, wearing jeans and a T-shirt that clung to his muscled torso, he sat in a high-backed swivel stool at the granite counter, Daniel in the curve of his arm.

The baby was staring up at him and sucking contentedly at a bottle of formula.

The two of them looked as if they'd been doing this kind of thing forever.

"Hey, buddy," Dante said, "you're doing a great job. That's the way. Drink it all down. I know it isn't what you're used to but it's good for you just the same. It'll put hair on your chest, you'll see."

Gabriella's eyes filled with tears. She leaned back against the wall, determined not to let Dante see her until she got herself under control. Seeing her lover—her once-upon-a-time lover—and her son like this was almost more than she could bear.

And yet she knew better than to read anything into the scene.

Dante was an intelligent, capable man. Faced with a problem, he would always attempt to solve it: she was sick; the baby needed to be cared for; he'd taken charge. He was good at that. Still, it was hard to see the two of them together without feeling almost indescribable joy.

"Okay, pal. What happens next?"

The baby gave an enormous burp. Dante laughed. "Well, that answers that question." Another huge burp. Dante grinned. "That good, huh? Hey, I'm a steak-and-potatoes guy myself but whatever floats your boat works for me. So, okay. Your belly's full. You don't look the least bit sleepy. You need a trip to the john? I'll bet you do. Well, let's give it a try—"

Gabriella took a breath and stepped briskly into the kitchen. Dante turned toward her, eyebrows lifting.

"Hey."

"Hey, yourself." She smiled. "Thank you for feeding the baby."

"Nothing to it," he said with just a touch of macho pride. "The doctor recommended this brand of formula and I had the pharmacy send up a case." He frowned. "But what are you doing out of bed? You were supposed to ring the bell if you needed me."

She held out her arms for the baby, who gave her a loopy grin.

"I know. But I thought a little exercise might do me good." The baby kicked its arms and legs. Gabriella smiled as she reached for him. "Besides," she said softly, "I missed you."

Fool that he was, Dante at first thought she was talking to him. She wasn't, of course, she was talking to Daniel. He realized it just in time to stop from saying that he had missed her, too.

But, dammit, he had.

It was a long time since she'd been here.

He'd always loved it when she'd stayed the night. It

hadn't happened often. She'd almost always refused to do it and he—well, he'd never been big on having women spend the night in his bed. It led to too many expectations.

But he'd loved having Gabriella stay here. Being able to reach for her, not just during the dark hours of night but in that quiet time just before dawn. Seeing her, first thing in the morning, looking the way she looked now, warm and tousled, wrapped in his robe, her hair brushed into a cloud of gold and chestnut, no makeup, no what Falco had dubbed the "*Five A.M. face*" women obviously put on while a guy was still sleeping.

The fact was, it was more than a year and he'd never had another woman here overnight. He hadn't wanted to, hadn't wanted anybody else in his bed or in his life for more than an evening.

Hell, he thought, and cleared his throat.

"Okay," he said brightly. "It's bathroom time. Hand the kid over."

Gabriella laughed. "He can't do 'bathroom time.' He's only a baby."

Dante gave her a look, then lifted the baby from her arms.

"She thinks I don't know that," he said to Daniel, who stared at him with solemnity. "Should we show her how wrong she is?"

"Dante, honestly—"

"She likes that word," he told the baby. "That word, 'honestly.' What she means when she says it is, 'Honestly, you men. You think you know everything.'" While he spoke, he was moving out of the kitchen, down the hall, to the stairs, the baby now making happy sounds, little trills of laughter. "Can you do the stairs?"

It took Gabriella a second to realize he meant her.

"Yes. Of course I can. But what…"

"No. Come to think of it, I don't trust you on the stairs. Not yet. So, you stay right there. I'll come back for you."

"Dante. Honestly—"

"Two 'honestlys' in one conversation." Dante shook his head, turned back to her and brushed his mouth lightly over hers. "Amazing."

She couldn't help laughing, even though she didn't want to. "No. I mean, honestly—"

He kissed her again, his lips lingering on hers, the baby between them cooing at this new, delightful game. When he drew back, he ran his hand along her cheek.

"That's the penalty," he said softly. "A kiss, each time you use that word. Now, stay put. Okay?"

She nodded. It was all she could manage.

He went up the stairs quickly, came down just as quickly but without the baby. She waited for a wail of protest and heard, instead, her son's contented gurgles.

Dante swept her into his arms. It felt—it felt wonderful. Hours ago he'd carried her up these same steps but she'd been too sick to enjoy it. Now she was aware of everything it entailed. The steady beat of his heart. The solid feel of his chest. The light pressure of his hand at the side of her breast. The clean, soap-and-water scent of his skin and hair.

The sweet pull of desire in her breasts and belly.

"You've lost weight."

His voice was gruff. She nodded.

"Maybe a little."

"What for? You were perfect, just the way you were."

Perfect. The word seemed to shimmer with light.

"I…it wasn't deliberate. I…I had a lot of things to do, when I got back to the *fazenda*."

"The baby." His tone grew even more gruff. "I'm sorry you had to go through that alone."

She thought of telling him that she had not been entirely alone, that her brother had been there for her, at least at the beginning. But that would only lead to questions. Dante didn't know anything about her brother; they'd always kept their talk impersonal. Intimate, yes. Dante had whispered things to her in bed. Things that had made her tremble with desire. With need. With…with what she felt for him.

"Here we go," he said, as he carried her through a door, not to his room but to one just across from it.

Gabriella's mouth fell open.

This was a baby's room.

Not in decor. The walls were cream; there were white-and-black vertical blinds at the windows, a black-and-white Scandinavian area rug underfoot. But it was furnished for a small child.

Winnie the Pooh smiled from atop a bird's-eye maple dresser, side by side with a baby monitor. A teddy bear with button eyes sat in the seat of a baby swing. A changing table stood against one wall, a big maple rocker against another. Facing her was surely the most beautiful crib in the whole world, also made of maple, fitted with sheets patterned with kittens and puppies. A mobile of rocket ships and suited spacemen amid stars, moons and planets hung over it.

Her son lay on his back in the crib, arms and legs going like mad, eyes fixed to the mobile, his face a portrait of delight.

"I didn't know what you'd like," Dante said. "So I just ordered some stuff."

She looked up at him. His mouth was a whisper away. *Say something,* her brain shrieked, but she couldn't come up with a single word.

Dante cleared his throat.

"Look, there's no problem with sending it all back. You know, if it's not what you wanted—"

"Oh, Dante! It's wonderful!"

His face cleared. "You think?"

"It's just that—" she hesitated "—we can't impose on you this way. I mean, I know how busy you are. Orsini Investments. Your family. The last thing you need is…is someone from the past cluttering up your life, your home—"

He silenced her the only way he could.

He kissed her. And kissed her. And when she kissed him back and sighed his name in the way that had always sent spirals of desire straight down to his toes, he knew that everything he had done—bringing her here, sweeping aside his plans to find her an apartment and instead settling her into his home, was right.

The idea had come to him while the doctor was with her. Gabriella was sick; she had the baby to care for. No way could he let her be on her own just yet. She'd simply have to stay with him for a couple of days. Just a temporary arrangement, of course, but even so, the baby would need things…

Except that now, looking down at the woman in his arms, he knew those were all pathetic rationalizations.

"I want you here," he said softly, when he finally ended the kiss. "Here. With me. You and the boy—you and Daniel belong here."

"Dante." Her voice shook. "Please. Don't say that and not mean it."

"We'll take things one step at a time."

It wasn't quite the answer her heart wanted but it was an honest answer. How could she fault him for that? she thought, and she nodded and said, very softly, "Okay."

He leaned his forehead against hers. "Starting with that bathroom stuff you were positive I couldn't handle."

She smiled into his eyes. "Somehow, I can't picture you changing a diaper."

"Who says? Put your money where your mouth is."

Her smile became a grin. "A buck says you can't."

"You're on."

She lost the bet.

Dante could do everything. Run a powerful corporation? Sure. Make every man in a room defer to him? That, too. Be the man all the women in the world wanted? Easy.

She'd known all that from experience.

What she'd never known until now was that he could diaper a baby as if he'd done it all his life. Take care of her. Brew her a cup of tea. Stand over her until she gave up and downed another couple of Tylenol. Whip up a meal—though as he pointed out, heating a can of chicken broth for her, taking a steak from the freezer and broiling it for himself wasn't exactly gourmet cooking. But it was much, much more than she'd ever seen him do in the past. Back then he'd been a whiz at making restaurant reservations and, once or twice, phoning down for Chinese take-out.

Dante Orsini, doing kitchen duty?

Never…until tonight.

Hours later she and Daniel were both yawning. Dante offered to give the baby a bottle but she said no, she'd nurse him. "Are you sure?" Dante said and she nodded and decided that telling him she really had to do it, that her breasts would be swollen and heavy unless she did, was more than she wanted to discuss. It was too private, too intimate…

Too much.

She nursed Daniel, sitting in the beautiful rocking chair in his room while Dante cleaned up the kitchen. When she was done, they bathed the baby together. Dante said he felt too clumsy to do it, but he took over halfway through, laughing when Daniel splashed water all over him, wrapping the baby in a big bath towel, then diapering him and dressing him in a blue onesie.

Dante lowered him gently into his crib. Gabriella kissed her son's head. Dante stroked his dark hair.

"Good night, pal," he said softly.

Out in the hall, for the first time all day, they were alone. The penthouse seemed wrapped in silence. Their eyes met. She felt the heat rise in her face. He took a step toward her. She took a quick step back.

"No. We can't." Her voice was breathless. "It would—it would only complicate things."

He nodded. Hadn't he already reached that same conclusion?

It was her turn to nod. "So…so, good night."

"Good night, sweetheart," he whispered. And then he reached for her and she went into his arms.

CHAPTER TEN

SHE went into his arms as if she had never left them.

A dozen thoughts raced through his head.

He wanted to tell her how he had missed her. How it felt to hold her again. But the need to kiss her, taste her, the need to possess her, make her his again had a hot urgency that drove away reason.

It was the same for her.

He could tell by the little sounds she made, the way she clung to his neck. By the motion of her body against his; that long, elegant body he had, yes, never forgotten.

And her mouth.

Sweet. Soft. Giving. A man could lose himself, just taking her mouth again and again, but it wasn't enough, not now, not after all these endless months. He drew her away from the door, backed her against the wall, tore open her robe and swept his hands over her silken skin. Her hands were on him, too, at his jeans, undoing the closure, unzipping him, and he groaned as she closed her hand around him and said his name in a broken whisper that almost drove him to his knees.

"Yes," he said, "yes, sweetheart."

He hooked his fingers in her panties. Eased them down. He knelt; she put a hand on his head to steady herself as she stepped free of the scrap of silk. He clasped her ankle. Rose to his feet, his hand moving up and up her leg. His touch was warm and possessive and it made her tremble.

"Open for me," he said in a strangled voice, and when she did, he put his hand between her thighs.

A cry burst from her throat. She was wet and hot for him, only for him, and he couldn't wait. Not anymore. He had wanted this without knowing it, waited for this for more than a year, and if he didn't have her now, he'd be lost forever.

He reversed their positions so that the wall was at his back. And as she sobbed his name, he lifted her, brought her down onto his rigid length. Her arms tightened around his neck, her legs wrapped around his waist. She buried her face against his throat and he could feel the heat of her breath, hear her breathy moans of ecstasy.

Too fast, his fevered brain told him, *dammit, too fast....*

She cried out. Sank her teeth into his flesh. And as she convulsed around him, Dante drove deep, rode her even harder, and flew off the edge of the world.

They stayed that way for long minutes, breathing hard, letting the aftermath of their passion ease. Then Gabriella gave a soft laugh. He remembered that laugh, low and delicious and earthy.

"What?" he said, his lips curving in a smile against her forehead.

"All those years of yoga that I took…" Another husky laugh. "Turns out they were worth it."

He grinned, let her down slowly. She looked up at him and she was so beautiful…the tightness in his chest almost overwhelmed him.

"Gabriella."

"Mmm?"

He shook his head. "Nothing," he said quietly, "just…" He bent his head and kissed her. Then he lifted her in his arms and carried her to his bed. She lay with her head on his shoulder, her hand playing with the dark curls on his chest.

"What are you thinking?"

Gently he stroked a tousled mass of golden curls from her cheek.

"That I've missed you."

She turned her face, pressed a kiss to his skin. "Me, too."

In truth he was thinking far more than that. He was thinking that a man went through life certain he knew what he needed to be happy. Success in his work. The love of his family. Friends who stood by him. Things that seemed simple and attainable.

It wasn't enough.

He needed this.

Gabriella, in his arms. Winding her arms around his neck as he gathered her closer, returning his kisses as if nothing in the world mattered but him.

He gathered her closer. How had he lived without her?

Without warning, a thought raced through him like a gust of cold air. *This could be dangerous.* There was so much to discuss, to work through. But then Gabriella sighed, kissed his throat and he knew that nothing mattered but her.

The swift tide of desire rose inside him again.

Kissing her, he rolled her onto her back, caught her hands in his and laced their fingers together. He drew back a little, just far enough to see her.

She was exquisite.

Her hair was a tangled mass of gleaming golds, her eyes were wide and luminous, her lips were softly swollen from his kisses. Everything had happened so quickly that she was still wearing his robe and, under it, his T-shirt. He bent his head, kissed her throat, the pulse racing wildly in its hollow. His tongue dipped into her mouth, capturing the honeyed sweetness he had never forgotten.

"Gabriella."

His voice was thick, his breathing ragged. He ached, not only to make love to her again but to see all of her. Gently he eased the robe from her shoulders and slid his hands under the hem of the shirt. Her skin felt like silk; the scent of her arousal made his blood pound even harder.

The back of his hand brushed against the soft curls between her thighs. She moaned; the sound inflamed him. Watching her face, he parted her labia with the tips of his fingers. Her head fell back, her lashes drooped over her eyes.

"Do you like it when I do this?" The words were thick, raw with need. "Gabriella? When I touch you here?"

"Yes," she sobbed, "yes, yes…"

His finger stroked her clitoris. It was the most perfect flower imaginable. He loved the feel of it, the desperate little sounds she made when he caressed it. But it wasn't enough. He wanted to kiss her belly, her breasts.

"Sweetheart," he whispered. "Sit up. Let me get this damned shirt out of the way…"

"Dante…"

"Just lift your arms and I'll—"

"Don't!" She caught his wrists, her eyes pleading with his. "Don't," she said unsteadily. "Please."

"What is it? What did I do? Gaby. Baby…" Hell! What a fool he was. He exhaled sharply, gathered her in his arms, kissed her temples, her eyelids, her mouth. "Forgive me. I should have realized. It's too much. You're sick…."

"No. Oh, no. I'm fine."

Even worse. Dante cursed himself for being a fool.

She'd had a baby only four months ago. He should have thought, should have asked.

"It's…it's—"

"The baby. Daniel. I understand. Just tell me I didn't hurt you because if I did, God, if I did—"

She put her fingers against his lips.

"No. It isn't that." She took a deep breath. "It's…it's that I've changed." She hesitated. "My breasts. My body." The tip of her tongue swiped lightly over her lips. "Maybe…maybe if you just leave the shirt—"

He silenced her with a kiss. "I want to see you," he whispered.

Gabriella shook her head. "My breasts aren't the way they used to be. And…and there are stretch marks on my belly."

He kissed her again, framing her face with his hands, then gently stroked her hair back from her face.

"You are the most beautiful woman in the world, sweetheart."

"No. I'm not. Having a baby changes things."

"Yes. It makes you a woman. My woman."

She offered a tremulous smile. "I know I must sound silly. But I don't want to disappoint you. I couldn't stand it if—"

"Gaby. How could you ever do that?" His mouth twisted. "I'm the one, not you. I disappointed you. I hurt you. I left you alone to face the hardest days in your life and—"

"You didn't know."

"But I do now. And I want to see you. Please…"

He waited, wondering how he would survive it if she refused him, knowing he would never force her to do anything even if it meant he had to spend the next twenty-four hours under a cold shower.

She took a breath. Nodded. And let go of his wrists.

Even more slowly, he drew the cotton T up, eased it carefully over her head. He could feel her trembling and he wanted to gather her in his arms, rock her against him, tell her she would always be perfect in his eyes whether she thought so or not.

He tossed the shirt aside. Her hands flew to her breasts. Dante shook his head and drew them away. He looked at her, and the breath caught in his throat.

She was more than beautiful, she was heart-stoppingly lovely.

Her breasts were fuller and all the more feminine for it. Her nipples, a pale pink that had always reminded him of summer roses, were a duskier shade than in the past.

His eyes moved down her body. The elegant indentation of her waist. Her belly, not flat but delicately convex and faintly, all but invisibly, striped with silver.

Yes, her body was changed. His seed, his son, had changed it. She was the essence of femininity.

And she was his.

Pride, primitive and male, the same emotions that must have driven the earliest man when he first emerged from his cave, swept through him. *Mine,* he thought, and he reached for her and brought her close against his heart within his encircling arms.

"Gabriella. You are exquisite."

"You don't have to say—"

He drew back. Kept his eyes on hers as he cupped a breast, traced the erect crest with a finger. She moaned; he thought he had never heard a more exciting sound.

"Your breasts are beautiful." He dropped his hand to her belly, curved his fingers over her warm flesh. "And this, your skin gilded with silver…" His gaze narrowed. "You are mine, sweetheart, and I have never wanted you more than I want you now."

He kissed her, parting her lips with his, kissed her throat, the slope of her breast, and when he drew the ruched pink tip into his mouth, her cry of pleasure shot through him. He teased her with his tongue. Licked. Nipped. Sucked… and suddenly there was a new taste, a taste even sweeter and richer—

Her hands flattened against his shoulders, pushed him away.

He lifted his head, saw panic in her eyes.

"I *am* hurting you," he said gruffly. "Baby, I told you. We'll stop—"

"You're not! The feel of your mouth is…is wonderful." Color leaped into her cheeks. "But I should have realized. I should have known. Sometimes, after I feed the baby, there's…there's a little milk still left. I should have warned you that…that—"

"Warned me?" He caught her wrists as she tried, again, to cover her breasts. "You're a woman, sweetheart. My woman. I love knowing that you can do this for Daniel." He paused. "For our son."

She gave a little sob, slid her hands into his hair, brought his lips to hers for a long, deep kiss and fell with him into the flames.

Dante stroked her breasts. Her belly. Her thighs. She cried out, sought his mouth. Her hand cupped his straining erection. The breath hissed through his teeth and he kicked free of his jeans.

Too fast. Way too fast. How could he, a man who was almost arrogant about his sexual control, how could he be so close to losing that control now? Because, dammit, he was.

He could feel the tightening in his scrotum, the

tension building in every muscle. He was racing to the edge, heart pounding, holding back, holding back, because his Gabriella deserved more. More of his mouth at her breasts. His hand between her thighs. His fingers parting her, finding her clitoris. More of this and this and this, he thought fiercely, as she cried out and arched off the bed.

"Please," she whispered, and he groaned, thrust into her. Deep. Hard. Fast. She reached up to him and he kissed her, rode her as she wrapped her legs around his waist.

"Dante," she sobbed. "Oh, Dante…"

She climaxed; he felt it happen, heard the trill of joy that broke from her throat, and he threw back his head and knew that what was happening to him had never happened before.

He was with her as they flew into the burning heart of the universe.

They slept in each other's arms, legs entwined, her head on his chest, his arm curved around her, his hand lightly cupping her breast.

And awoke to the darkness of the night, the wonder of being together, the sweetness of it.

The deep, hungry need for fulfillment.

He caressed her. Feathered his fingertips over her nipples. Kissed them. Stroked his hand down her body, between her legs, sought and found the very heart of her.

She moaned. Arched against his seeking hand. Used every feminine motion of her body to beg him for more. Still he hesitated. All the mysteries of a woman's body after childbirth, he had learned tonight. She said he couldn't hurt her, but for all he knew, in his ignorance, he could. Making love more than once, God, more than twice, might be a mistake.

"Are you sure you can do this?" he said, his lips a breath from hers.

She gave that wonderful laugh again, wrapped her hand around him and said, "You tell me."

He growled, rolled her on her back, lifted her leg and brought it high over his, opening her to him but entering her as slowly as he could bear.

It was agony.

Exquisite agony.

So was her soft moan of pleasure.

A shudder gripped his powerful body; he buried his face in her throat as he filled her, deeper, deeper, until he couldn't tell where he ended and she began. Until they were one. One, he thought, his heart filling with joy…

And then she moved.

His mind emptied.

She moved again and he groaned, moved with her and she cried out, sank her teeth into his shoulder and they let go together, shattered together, fell off the edge of the world together.

He held her until her breathing eased and he knew she was asleep. Then he kissed her, checked the baby monitor, smiled at the sight of his sleeping son. He drew the duvet over them both, gathered her close again.

He had never felt so complete in his life.

He slept, too.

They woke. Made love. The moon rose and set. And the night slipped away and became morning.

Gabriella opened her eyes to the soft patter of rain.

Rain, this time of year? It was too soon. Rainy season didn't come to the Pantanal until—

But she wasn't in the Pantanal. She was in Manhattan. In Dante's home.

In Dante's bed.

Memories of the long, incredible night rushed in. She tried to remember how many times they'd made love even as she chastised herself for the effort. It didn't matter... But, somehow, it did. Dante had always been an amazing lover. Tender. Savage. Giving and demanding all at once. Indefatigable. She'd been with only a couple of men before meeting him, so she was far from an expert. Still, Dante's virility was, well, amazing.

And yet last night the frequency with which he'd wanted her had shocked her.

She had wanted him, too, each time. And that had shocked her, as well, that her need for him had seemed insatiable, her desire for him endless. But then, it had always been that way with him. She'd always wanted him; even these past endless months, unable to imagine feeling a need for sex ever again, even then, if she were honest, there'd been nights she'd dreamed of Dante. Hot dreams. Dreams from which she'd awakened empty and shaken, an ache low in her belly, her breasts full and sore...

Her breasts, full and sore...

Deus! The baby! She shot a look at the baby monitor, but it showed only an empty crib. Quickly she rose from the bed. Dante's robe, the one she'd worn yesterday, was neatly draped over the back of a chair. She yanked it on, hurried to Daniel's room...

And saw Dante by the window, holding his son in his arms.

He smiled when he saw her. "Good morning, sweetheart."

"I overslept. I don't know how. The baby—"

"He's fine." He looked down. "Aren't you, buddy?"

Daniel offered an enormous grin. Dante did the same. "See? He's great."

"He must be starving…"

"Well, we were starting to think we'd have to wake you. I mean, a snack's a snack but when a guy wants his breakfast…"

"What snack?"

"He woke up at five."

"You mean, I slept through it?"

Dante smiled. "Yeah," he said huskily. "Imagine that."

She blushed, tore her eyes from his and looked at the clock. Jack and Jill were going up the hill, carrying a huge wristwatch instead of a pail of water. Her mouth fell open.

"Ten?" she said, bewildered. "It's ten in the morning?"

"It's okay. I gave him a bottle at six." Dante gave a modest shrug but it was impossible not to notice the self-satisfied smile on his face. "I diapered him, too." He shuddered. "It was, uh, an interesting experience."

She really tried not to laugh but a giggle escaped, and then another, and finally she was guffawing at the thought of her sophisticated, urbane lover changing a diaper full of poo.

Her lover, she thought, and her laughter faded. Dante was her lover again, her foolish heart was in his hands.

"Hey," he said softly, "honey, what is it?"

"Nothing," she said, and forced a smile. "Here. Give me the baby. I'll feed him."

Daniel went into her arms. She sat down in the rocker, started to open her robe…and hesitated.

"May I stay?"

Dante's voice was low and soft. No, Gabriella thought, no, he could not stay. Every act of intimacy would be that much more difficult to forget after this time together ended. This was temporary. Dante might want her in his bed but the rest—permanency, fatherhood…

"Gaby? Sweetheart, if you want me to leave—"

"No," she said, in rushed whisper. "Please. Don't go. Stay with us."

The look that swept across his face made her want to weep with happiness. He kissed her upturned face, then sat down on the floor, cross-legged. She opened her robe. The baby turned his head, latched hungrily on to her nipple. She smiled at her son, then at her lover.

And knew that this time, when Dante left her, there would be nothing left of her heart.

CHAPTER ELEVEN

IF THERE was one thing all the Orsini brothers knew, it was that no one walked a straight path through life.

There were sideroads and missteps, deep currents that threatened to suck a man under, chasms that might take a lifetime to bridge.

All the Orsinis had experienced those things.

It was how Rafe had ended up in the Army, Nick in the Marines, Falco in Special Forces. It was how Dante had found himself in the far reaches of Alaska, doing dangerous work in the oil fields. It was, in the end, how all four of them had returned to New York, taking one hell of a deep brotherly breath and invested everything—Nick's and Rafe's savings, Falco's poker winnings and Dante's fat oil field paychecks—in what had eventually become one of the most successful private investment firms in the world.

Chasms. Deep currents. Put bluntly, jumping in with your eyes closed.

That was what Dante was thinking Monday morning, as he shaved.

He'd done that this weekend. Bringing Gabriella and Daniel to New York was one thing. Moving them into his life was another. And, yeah, he had done that, changing a guest room into a nursery, moving Gabriella from the guest suite into the master suite. She'd protested, come up with all kinds of reasons it was a mistake, and maybe because a tiny piece of him worried she might be right, he'd swept her into his arms, kissed her concerns away and switched her clothes, her makeup, all her stuff, from her room to his.

Chasms and currents, all right. And, sure, sometimes you didn't make it, but sometimes you did. And when you did… Dante smiled, turned on the water, cupped it in his hand and rinsed away the last dollops of shaving cream.

When you did, man, life was terrific.

He reached for a towel, dried off as he looked around his bathroom. A day ago it had been an austere male kingdom. Nothing on top of the long marble counter except his shaving brush, an electric razor he hardly ever used, a plain comb and brush. Everything else was in the deep drawers of the vanity. Now, little glass vials and jars, a perfume bottle, a mother-of-pearl-backed hairbrush and half a dozen other things stood on the countertops.

He ran a fingertip lightly over the hairbrush where a few strands of gold glittered among the soft bristles.

It was Gabriella's stuff. He loved seeing it here and wasn't that a hell of thing coming from a guy who had to count to ten if some woman left a tube of lipstick behind?

But Gaby was not "some woman." She was…she was special. Beautiful. Bright. Sexy. It had rained yesterday and they'd ended up spending most of it before the fireplace, reading the *Times,* tackling the crossword puzzle together. The baby, Daniel, lay on the antique Rya rug between them, cooing and smiling, kicking his arms and legs, suddenly sobbing as if his small heart would break.

"What?" Dante had said, panicked.

"He's hungry," Gabriella had replied, smiling, and she'd nursed him right there, sitting in the curve of Dante's arm, and what he'd felt, watching the baby at the breast of his woman, had almost overwhelmed him.

It had been her turn to look at him, raise her eyebrows and say, "What?"

"Nothing," he'd told her, because what happened to him when he saw her nurse the baby was too much to put into words.

Their baby.

Daniel was his.

He knew it, had known it from the start. There was no question about it. That path, the one that led through life, was, for once, straight as an arrow. He and Gabriella had been lovers, he'd made her pregnant and absolutely the road was straight...

Straight as the road that ended at a house surrounded by a white picket fence, a station wagon, a dog and a cat and...

"Dante?"

A light tap at the door startled him.

"Yes," he said. His voice sounded strange, even to him, and he cleared his throat and tried again. "Yes. Okay. Just give me a couple of minutes."

"I have a quick question."

"Yeah, well, like I said, can you wait a minute?"

Merda. He winced as the impatient words left his lips.

"Never mind. I didn't mean to disturb you—"

Ah, God, he was worse than an idiot, he thought, yanking the door open, reaching for Gabriella and drawing her into his arms even as she turned away.

"How could you ever disturb me?" he said gruffly.

"No, really, it is all right."

The hell it was. He'd hurt her; he could see it in her eyes.

"Confession time," he said, cupping her face, tilting it to his. "I am not a morning kind of guy."

The faintest of smiles tugged at the corners of her lips. "You were always a morning kind of guy," she said softly. "And you just proved it again a little while ago."

He grinned at the compliment. "Being that kind of morning guy is easy."

Her smile dimmed just a little. "I'm sure."

"Hey." Gently he threaded his fingers through her hair. "Maybe you need to know I've never asked a woman to move in with me until now."

Her eyes searched his. "Is that what you've done? Asked me to move in?"

That straight path, leading to that white picket fence, that house...

Dante blanked the picture from his mind. "Yes," he said, and kissed her.

Long moments later she sighed. "I know I had a reason for coming in here."

"Mmm," he said, slipping his hand down the back of her jeans.

"I know what it— Dante. How can I think if you...if you—"

"You have," he said solemnly, stilling the motion of his hand, "one minute for thinking."

"I'd like to tell Mrs. Janiseck to add baby cereal to her shopping list. The doctor in Bonito said I could add it to Daniel's diet when he seemed ready, and—"

"So tell her."

"Well, I was going to but she's your housekeeper and—"

"You don't have to clear things with me, honey. Just tell Mrs. Janiseck whatever you want to tell her. Come to think of it..." He took his wallet from the back pocket of his trousers, slid out a credit card and pressed it into her hand. "I should have thought of this sooner."

"No. I cannot permit you to—"

"And *I* cannot permit *you* to argue with me," he said gently. "The card is yours, Gabriella. Buy whatever you like. For the baby, for yourself. Whatever you need or want."

She looked at the card, then at him. "A loan, then. Until I am back on my feet."

He didn't want her on her feet, he wanted her in his bed, he thought, and felt heat sweep through his body.

"What?"

"Nothing. You and Mrs. Janiseck doing okay?"

"Oh, yes. She's wonderful."

Wonderful, indeed. His housekeeper hadn't so much as blinked at finding a woman and baby in his life; if anything, she'd seemed delighted.

"She has a niece, did you know that?"

"No. No, I didn't."

"Stacia. She is studying to be a teacher. She's been an *au pair* the last few summers. Mrs. Janiseck says she's excellent with babies. She suggested she could stay with Daniel—when I am out on interviews."

This entire conversation was starting to sail over his head.

"Interviews?"

"Yes. I telephoned my old agent and asked him to see if he can get me some work. Why are you frowning? I need work, Dante. I have no money and…and I already owe you a fortune."

He supposed she did need to work. Not to repay him for anything; he'd never take a dime from her, but instinct told him not to tell her that just now. But, yes, she needed to work for the same reason he did, for the fulfillment of it— except, she could feel all that, the fulfillment of just being with him. He was sure of it because it was how he felt, being with her, and what in hell was he doing, heading for the office after only a handful of days alone with his Gabriella?

"I have," he said, "a brilliant idea."

She gave a soft laugh. "Such modesty."

"We'll tell Mrs. Janiseck we'll hire Stacy—"

"Stacia."

"We'll ask Stacia if she'd like to be Daniel's nanny. I'm sure we can work out a schedule flexible enough to suit her."

"Yes, but—"

"But," he said solemnly, "you can't afford it."

She flushed. "No. I can't."

"Well, you won't have to. See, I'll employ her, not you."

"I cannot impose on you this way, Dante."

"I need the tax break," he said, lying with aplomb. Who even knew if a nanny's wages were deductible? More to the point, who gave a damn?

"So many tax breaks," she said, raising her eyebrows. "The *fazenda,* a nanny—"

His mouth captured hers. His hand delved deeper, cupping her bottom, seeking her sweet heat. She caught her breath, rose to him, wrapped her arms around his neck.

"Dante," she whispered, her lips an inch from his, "we have to talk."

He answered by scooping her into his arms, saying to hell with the office and carrying her back to bed.

An hour later he phoned his AP, told her he wouldn't be in for the week.

"Still out of town," she said, because he was using his cell and one of the best things about cells was that they didn't give away your location. "Want to give me an alternate phone number or stay with your mobile?"

"The mobile," he said casually.

It wasn't as if he were avoiding telling her he was home. Or telling his brothers. It was just that he didn't feel like explaining things just yet to them or, God forbid, his sisters and his mother. The situation—that word again—was still complicated. While he worked things out, it was probably best to keep the news about Gabriella and the baby to himself.

A man was entitled to privacy, wasn't he? Besides, he hadn't taken any time off in months.

He asked Mrs. Janiseck to invite her niece over for an interview. Stacia showed up late morning. She was charming; she had great references and when she took Daniel from Gabriella's arms, he gave her a solemn look and said, "Ba-ba-ba-ba!"

"Oh, he's babbling," Gabriella said happily. "Right on time!"

Dante felt like asking why babbling was such a big deal. He did it all the time—but he had a feeling the three women would have given him the kind of look a man did not want women to give, so he nodded wisely.

"Such a big, beautiful boy," Stacia cooed.

He could actually see the tension ease from Gabriella's shoulders.

"Okay, sweetheart," he said softly. "How about we go out for lunch?"

"Do, please," Stacia said. "That will give Daniel and me time to get acquainted."

Gabriella and Stacia talked about diapers. About formula. About a zillion things until, finally, Mrs. Janiseck clucked her tongue and shooed Dante and Gabriella gently out the door.

"Just go," she said softly. "Enjoy being together." And to Dante's amazement, she rose as high as she could in her sturdy black orthopedic shoes, grabbed his face, hauled it down to hers and planted a kiss on his cheek.

It was the kind of perfect fall day that made New Yorkers forget the hot, sticky summers and the bone-chilling winters when the snow turned into gray slush. Arms around each other, Dante and Gabriella strolled through Central Park.

She commented happily on everything. Babies. Runners. An elderly couple holding hands. People walking, and being walked by, their dogs. There was no need to ask his Gaby if she liked dogs. By the time she'd stopped to pet at least a hundred of them—okay, a slight exaggeration but not by much—by then, even he could tell that she didn't like dogs, she loved them.

When she got to her feet after a conversation with a miniature schnauzer, Dante asked the obvious question.

"Did you have a lot of dogs when you were a kid?"

She looked at him in surprise. "Oh, I never had a dog."

It was his turn to look surprised. "No dogs? On that big ranch?"

She gave a little shrug. "My father did not like dogs."

"Why not?"

Another little shrug. And, perhaps, a tiny hesitation. And then, "He just did not like them."

Something was up. Her English was taking on that just-learned-it nuance. Dante took her hand, decided to take the conversation in a new direction.

"I wanted a dog like crazy when I was growing up."

She smiled at him. "But your mother said no, no dogs in an apartment."

Had he never told her he'd grown up in a house? There was an awful lot they didn't know about each other, he thought, lacing their fingers together.

"I grew up in a house. A pretty big one, in the Village."

"But still, no dog?"

He shrugged. "Mama was convinced dogs would give us germs."

"Mama," Gabriella said, smiling.

"We're Sicilian." Dante grinned. "Calling her anything else might have won me a smack."

"And your father is Papa?"

His smile disappeared. "I never call him Papa, or Dad, or anything but Father."

"Hey. I'm sorry I—"

"No." He brought her hand to his lips and pressed a kiss to the palm. "You have a right to ask. The thing is, he's…he's—"

"Old-fashioned?"

"Old-country." A deep breath. She would surely know some of this from having read it in the papers; she'd even tossed that *famiglia* insult at him, but talking about it—that was something he never did. "Remember that Marlon Brando movie? My old man's kind of like that. The head of what he likes to refer to as a big company but in reality—"

"Dante." Gabriella stepped in front of him, laid a hand on his chest. "I don't care what he is," she said softly. "I am simply grateful that he gave you life."

Could you really feel your heart lift? The answer seemed to be yes, and right there, under the arch in the Ramble, he took Gabriella in his arms and kissed her.

Where else to take her for lunch on such a glorious day but The Boathouse?

It was early autumn but the temperature was in the low 70s, the sun was bright. Perfect for dining on the outdoor terrace beside the Central Park boat lake.

There were no tables available—but, yes, of course, there was a table for Mr. Orsini. Gabriella sat back, watching the turtles sunning themselves on a rocky outcropping. He ordered for both of them. Tuna Niçoise for her—he remembered she loved it—and a burger, well-done, for him.

"And a bottle of Pinot Grigio," he added, remembering she loved that, too, but she shook her head, glanced at the waiter, blushed and told Dante, in a low voice, that she couldn't drink because alcohol wouldn't be good for the baby.

The waiter gave a discreet smile. "Sparkling water, perhaps," he said, and Dante said yes, that would be fine.

The bottle of water arrived, along with glasses filled with ice and slices of lemon. Dante reached for Gabriella's hand.

"I wish I'd been with you when you were pregnant," he said softly. "And when you delivered. You shouldn't have been alone."

Gabriella shook her head. "I told you, I wasn't alone. Yara was there." She paused. "And my brother."

Dante watched her face, the sudden play of emotion in her eyes. "You know," he said carefully, "you never talk about him."

"There isn't much to say." Her voice trailed off; her eyes met his. There was a sudden fierce glow in them. "He is dead, but I suppose you know that."

"Sweetheart. I didn't want to make you sad. If you don't want to tell me—"

"He died of AIDS." The glow in her eyes grew even more fierce. "He was a good man, Dante. A wonderful brother."

"I'm sure he was," Dante said gently.

"Our father despised him." She gave a bitter laugh. "But

then, he despised me, too. My brother, because he was gay. Me, because I killed my mother."

"Gaby. Honey—"

The waiter arrived with their lunch. They fell silent until he'd left. Neither of them reached for a fork. At last Gabriella picked up her story.

"She died in childbirth, and our father said it was my fault." Dante clasped her hand; she gave his a tight squeeze. "I know how wrong that is now, but when I was a little girl, I believed it. Anyway, just about the time you and I—about the time we stopped seeing each other—"

"The time you found out you were carrying my baby," Dante said gruffly.

Another nod of her head. "*Sim.* My father wrote to me, a very conciliatory letter asking me to return home. He was getting old, he said, it was time to mend our relationship, he said…" She swallowed dryly. "So, considering that… that I wanted to leave New York, I went home. But he had lied to me. He was dying. He had no money—my father was a very heavy gambler. He needed someone to take care of him." She shrugged. "So I did."

"Ah, sweetheart, I'm so sorry. You needed someone to take care of you and instead—"

"I did not mind. There are things one must do in life." She lifted her head and smiled, though now there were tears in her eyes. "And a good thing came of it. I told my father I would only stay with him if he permitted my brother to move back in. Arturo was ill by then." She swallowed hard. "So Arturo and I were together again. It was wonderful. We talked and laughed and shared memories—and then my father died." Her voice broke. "And before very long, so did Arturo. And while I was still mourning him, Andre Ferrantes came to the door to tell me the bank was going to foreclose on Viera y Filho—my father had named the ranch at my brother's birth, you see, long before he could have known Arturo would be gay. And Ferrantes said— He said—"

Dante stood, pulled back her chair and kissed her. Then he drew her to her feet, dropped some bills on the table and led her from the terrace toward the door.

"How romantic," he heard a woman say.

And he thought, *Wrong*.

This, whatever was happening between them, was far more complicated than romance. It was…it was—

He clasped Gabriella's hand and hurried her from the park.

At home again, they checked on the baby.

He was sound asleep, his backside in the air.

Mrs. Janiseck left. So did Stacia. Dante took Gabriella out on the terrace. They sat close together on a love seat, his arm curved around her in the warm sun, surrounded by Izzy's flowers.

He told her all about his life. Things he'd never told anyone. His confused feelings for Cesare. His love for his brothers. For his sisters. He told her how lost he'd been at eighteen, how filled with rage because he had a father whose idea of *famiglia* had little to do with the family sitting around a dinner table and everything to do with some alien family whose existence periodically brought reporters and photographers and cops to the door.

He told her how directionless he'd been, how his brothers had said enlisting in one of the armed services would give his life structure—and how he'd known, instinctively, he needed the opportunity to find that structure in a different way.

He picked up her hand, kissed her fingertips and explained that he'd found it in Alaska, risking his not-so-precious neck in the oil fields, hiking alone whenever he could in the wilderness, camping out and watching the northern lights, listening to the mournful howl of the wolves until, at last, he'd seen his anger at life for the pettiness it was.

"So I flew home," he said. "To New York. And my brothers were starting to feel as directionless as I'd felt, now that Nick was out of the Marines, Rafe out of the Army and Falco was out of whatever in hell they had him doing in Special Forces."

And, he said, they spent hours talking. Planning. Ultimately pooled their savings and their areas of expertise in finance, where they all had done well in school and, in Falco's case, at the poker tables.

"Orsini Investments took off," he said. It still was doing well—an understatement, really, making their investors happy despite the slowed economy.

And finally he told her why he'd gone to Brazil, Cesare's bizarre request—and then the truth that he'd kept from facing.

He had gone there knowing he would not leave without searching for, and finding, her.

When he fell silent, Gabriella smiled, though her cheeks were damp with tears.

"Dante," she whispered, "Dante, *meu querido…*"

He drew her into his lap. They kissed. And touched. And when that was no longer enough, he took her to his bedroom, undressed her as slowly as if he were unwrapping a perfect gift.

An eternity later, with her lover still deep inside her as she lay sated in his arms in the afterglow of their passion, Gabriella finally faced the truth.

No matter what happened, she would always be in love with Dante Orsini.

CHAPTER TWELVE

IT WAS decades since Dante had played hooky.

He'd done it a lot in high school. Got into trouble for it, ended up on suspension once but school was dull and the world was exciting and, besides, even the principal had to admit he was too smart a kid to dump.

Or maybe the influence on the principal was fear of his old man.

Either way, he'd cut classes years back then and, yeah, at NYU, but ditching university classes wasn't the same thing, especially when you could ace the coursework without half trying.

But once he'd had his seemingly useless economics degree in hand and headed for Alaska, those easy days ended. He'd not only shown up at his job each day, he'd worked his ass off, too.

The idea had been to test himself. Get the wild streak that had driven him north out of his system. And to make a lot of money. He'd done that, too, though he'd never been quite sure why it had seemed so important except to know it represented freedom. Total and complete independence, even more so after he'd come home, invested what he'd saved along with his brothers in the company they'd started.

So, eventually, he had it all.

Freedom. Independence. And a lot of money. More money than he'd ever imagined, enough to buy pretty much anything the world had that he might possibly want.

And yet, Dante thought as he drew Gabriella into his arms on the dance floor of a tiny club in the East Village, and yet he had never truly realized that what a man most wanted carried no price tag at all.

Not just a man.

Him.

How could life change so fast? Ten days ago, ask him what made him happy and he'd have said, well, his work. His family. The call last night telling him there was a '58 Ferrari Berlinetta coming on the market in Palm Beach. And women, of course. An entire BlackBerry of them. Redheads, blondes, brunettes, all beautiful, all fun, all exciting.

For a little while, anyway.

The music went from fast to slow and easy. Not that it mattered. From the second they'd hit the dance floor, he'd held Gabriella close, his arms tightly around her, her arms around his neck, her face buried against his throat.

The truth was, nothing was as exciting as this. Gabriella, in his arms. In his life.

How could he ever have been foolish enough to have let her go?

She made him happy. And he made her happy. She'd gone from fragile and looking as if she were made of glass that might shatter, as she had in Brazil, to the woman she had been in the past. Smiling. Full of life. More beautiful than seemed possible.

She was her own woman.

And she was his.

He awoke to her softly whispered "Good morning," fell

asleep with her in his arms. He was never without her. They talked about everything under the sun, agreed on some things, agreed to disagree on others. They read the papers over breakfast, drove out to Long Island and walked the beach at Fire Island, empty and beautiful on a cool fall day.

At first Gabriella would remind him that they'd hired Stacia so she could get in touch with her agent, have him line up some interviews...

"Could that be better than this?" he'd ask her softly, and her answer was always in her kiss.

Sometimes they didn't talk at all. They just were together. He'd never before been with a woman and found the silence between them comfortable and easy.

And then there was Daniel.

He still didn't know much about kids, but even he could tell that the little guy was, well, one fine-looking baby. And, better still, brilliant. Those ba-ba-ba's had grown to include ga-ga-ga's. The kid would probably talk before he was a year old. Plus, the way he reached for that mobile above his crib, watched it with such obvious curiosity... Oh, yeah. Daniel was smart, and not only because he was his.

Which he was. Absolutely. How could he have ever doubted it?

"Dante?"

This had been the best week of his life. He was happy. Such a simple word, especially from a man who'd never thought much about his feelings, but—

"Dante!"

He blinked, looked down into Gabriella's smiling face. "What?" he said, and she gave a soft little laugh.

"We're still dancing."

"And?"

"And," she said, "the music stopped about five minutes ago."

She was right. They were alone on the dance floor, locked in each other's arms, people watching them and smiling.

"Amazing, because I could swear it's still playing."

Gabriella smiled. "Me, too."

Dante grinned, spun her in a circle, then dipped her back over his arm.

"You are *doido*," she said, laughing.

"*Doido* for you," he told her, dancing her to their table, snatching up her pashmina shawl, then waltzing her out the door. His driver spotted them almost instantly, rolled out of the No Parking zone where he'd been waiting and pulled to the curb. Dante signaled him to stay put, opened the passenger door himself and handed Gabriella inside. "Let's go home," he said. The driver nodded, closed the privacy partition and headed uptown as Gabriella snuggled into the curve of Dante's arm.

"Did you have a good time?" he said, pressing a kiss to her temple.

"Mmmm. A wonderful time." She smiled. "We'll try *salsa* next."

Dante gave a mock groan. "You just want to see me make a jerk of myself on the dance floor."

"Stop fishing for compliments, *senhor*. You're a fine dancer."

"*Salsa* means moving parts of the human body never meant to be moved."

A playful glint came into her eyes. "Ah, but I have seen you move those parts exceedingly well."

Dante drew her onto his lap. "But not on a dance floor," he said, his voice suddenly husky.

Gabriella threaded her hands into his hair and drew his face to hers.

"Perhaps we should test those moves when we get home," she whispered.

What a good thing a privacy petition was, Dante thought, and then he stopped thinking about anything but the woman in his arms.

Saturday morning, early, a courier delivered a package.

Dante insisted Gabriella watch as he opened it.

It was a long length of woven fabric with an adjustable closure. "It's a baby sling," he said, as he draped it over his shoulder and arm, then snugged Daniel securely within its soft folds. "I researched it online. Seems lots of tribal people have carried babies this way for centuries. It gives the babies a real sense of security. What do you think?"

"I think it's a great idea," she said, but what she really thought was that she was living a miracle.

The man who'd been one of New York's wildest bachelors, who had not even suspected he had a son less than two weeks ago, had become the world's most amazing father.

"You mean it?" He grinned as Daniel cooed. "Daniel, my man, what do you think?"

The baby laughed. So did Gabriella. Dante looked at her and smiled.

"I guess the vote's unanimous."

It was. She and her son both adored this man—but she couldn't tell him that. Not until he said the words she longed to hear. Instead she kissed the baby, rose on her toes and kissed her lover, too.

"Unanimous," she said brightly.

"Okay. Let's take it for a trial run. How's a trip to the Bronx Zoo sound?"

It sounded perfect, she told him. Dante smiled, handed

Daniel to her and put aside the baby sling. "Let me just check my e-mail. I haven't looked at it all week and Monday, much as I hate to do it, I'm going to have to go to work."

Her face fell; he loved the fact that it did. She didn't want him to leave. Hell, he didn't want it, either, but life had to return to normal sometime.

"Five minutes," he said softly, kissing her. "Not a second more, I promise."

But he was in his study longer than that and when he came out, she knew something had happened.

"Dante? Is everything all right?"

He assured her that it was.

It was not. His expression was closed; he was unusually silent during the drive to the zoo. Preoccupied, but by what?

Dante carried the baby in the sling as they made their way from exhibit to exhibit. He spoke to him the way he always did, as if the little guy understood every word he said about the seals and the monkeys and the giraffes.

But his behavior was subdued.

It was unsettling.

Eventually they took a break. Daniel had fallen asleep; Dante stood staring off into the distance, one hand curved around the baby, the other tucked in the pocket of his leather windbreaker.

He was quiet, his eyes impossible to read.

Gabriella felt her throat constrict.

Something was happening. What? It was as if the Dante who had gone into his study this morning had emerged a different person. He had changed. Everything had changed. She could feel it.

What if he'd decided he'd had enough? The zoo was

filled with families. Was it a graphic lesson in what his life had become?

She and the baby were both novelties. It was a crude way to put it but it was accurate. He'd never had a son before, and he'd never had a woman live with him, either. He'd made it sound like something wonderful when he'd told her that, but viewed with clinical detachment, it simply meant this experience was new for him.

Ocean kayaking had once been new to him, and back-country skiing and probably a dozen other things. Oh, she knew he cared far more for the baby than for any of that, but still, "newness" intrigued him.

It wasn't that he was self-indulgent. Or perhaps he was, just a little. It made him seem larger than life. It was one of his charms.

It also meant he was the kind of man who grew bored easily.

He'd told her that himself, just yesterday, though not in those exact words, when he'd gotten a call telling him some much-coveted kind of automobile was for sale some-where out of state. His excitement had been palpable; he'd whooped with glee, caught her up in his arms and kissed her, and when she'd laughed and said only a man could get so worked up over a car, he'd tried to explain how it was, that he loved fast cars, that he'd been hunting after this one for a long time. And that was when he'd mentioned kayaking and skiing and all the rest, how he'd loved them and more or less still did but how cars like this one had sup-planted his interest in other things.

Daniel had awakened just then, fussing for his dinner, so the conversation had ended before she could ask him the reason. Not that she had to ask.

She knew the reason.

Tides changed but the ocean was still the ocean.

Snowfall changed, but a mountain was still a mountain. Not so with automobiles. They were always different. When you grew bored with one kind, there was always another to pursue.

Was she his latest acquisition? Even more vital, was Daniel? Would her son learn to love his father only to have Dante turn into a stranger?

The thought terrified her.

Dante felt the warm weight of his sleeping son pressed against his chest.

He curved his hand over the child's bottom. He loved holding his son. The baby was so small, so trusting. He'd never imagined being a father could make a man's heart swell with pride and joy.

The zoo was full of families. Mothers, fathers, babies, kids of all ages. And them. He. Gabriella. Daniel. They were a family, too.

It was wonderful.

It was scary as hell.

And it had made him finally face the truth. Well, this— and the e-mail messages he'd found in his in-box. It was all he could think about. What was happening to Rafe…

What he was finally ready to admit was happening to him.

Had already happened to him.

Dear God, how could a man fall so hard, so fast? How could he have been blind to it? Gabriella had to feel the same way. She had to, because if she didn't…

He had to be alone with her. Take her in his arms. Tell her. Tell her—

"Gaby," he said abruptly, turning toward her, looking at the woman who held his life in her hands, "I know there's lots more to see, but—"

"Dante." Her eyes met his. "Please," she said in an unsteady whisper, "I would like to go home."

Mrs. Janiseck was off on Saturdays. So was Stacia.

As soon as they were alone, Dante cleared his throat. "Gabriella. We have to talk."

Her heart fell. "All right," she said tonelessly.

He flashed a quick smile. "I'll, ah, I'll put Daniel to bed. Why don't you, ah, why don't you start supper?"

She nodded, went into the kitchen. Actually, there was little to do. Mrs. Janiseck did almost all the cooking. Cold roast chicken and a green salad, prepared yesterday. There it was, on the top shelf in the fridge. Lovely to have it waiting, but somehow—and Gabriella knew how ridiculous the thought was—somehow, it made her feel even more a guest in Dante's life. Yes, of course, a woman to whom he had a permanent commitment would have a housekeeper and cook. Dante's income, his lifestyle, meant the woman to whom he had such a permanent commitment would have a staff to help run her home. But a woman to whom he had…

Gabriella laughed out loud, though it wasn't a happy sound.

What kind of phrase was that? 'A woman to whom he had…' Was there no word to describe what she should be to him? Not his mistress. Mistresses didn't come equipped with babies, and besides, a mistress was a woman whose lover owned the roof over her head, the food on her table, the clothes on her…

Which was exactly what she had become.

She closed the refrigerator door with a slam and went out to the terrace. It was cold outside. The city was wrapped in darkness and you could not only sense winter coming, you could feel it in the marrow of your bones.

Dante paid all her bills. Food. Daniel's clothing. Diapers. The furniture in the nursery. The rent or the mortgage, whatever it was. He paid for her clothes—she'd left so much at the *fazenda,* and she'd needed warmer things after arriving here.

It would take her years, a lifetime, to pay him back, even if her agent lined up the kind of modeling deals supermodels got, and the truth was, she'd been a successful model but not one who earned six figures a day.

He owned everything in her life and her son's life.

How had she let such a thing happen? What had become of her independence? Her sense of autonomy? Her determination, from childhood on, to rely on nobody but herself?

What had become of her responsibility to Daniel?

He deserved stability. Security. Not just financial security but the kind that came from the heart. A father's heart. She, of all people, knew how much that meant. Daniel was only a baby but already he smiled and laughed when Dante reached for him. Another few months, ba-ba-ba would turn into ma-ma-ma and da-da-da, but would Dante be there for him? Would he be there for her?

She took a deep breath. The word of the day was *commitment.*

As in forever. As in a man and a woman who were building a life together.

As in—

"Married," Dante said, and she spun toward him, heart pounding.

"What?"

He was smiling but the smile was a lie. She could see it in his eyes, the set of his mouth.

"My brother Rafe." He dug his hands into his trouser pockets as he stood beside her, his gaze on the skyline beyond the park and not on her. "When I checked my e-mail this morning, I found a couple of notes. Seems he's getting married tomorrow. Well, it turns out he's already married, some kind of quickie deal that happened in Sicily, and tomorrow, he's doing it for real. Meaning, in church where my mother can get all misty-eyed over it."

He sounded as if he were describing an *auto-da-fé* rather than a wedding but then, being burned at the stake might seem more appealing to a man like him. Was that why he'd been so distant all day?

"Oh," she said, because she had to say something. "Well, that's…that's—"

"He's been trying to reach me. The whole family has. But I've been out of touch."

He made it sound like an accusation. Gabriella narrowed her eyes.

"I did not keep you from checking your messages."

"Yeah, but who would ever expect a message like this?" Dante ran his hands through his shower-damp hair; it stood up in little black peaks. "I mean, this is crazy. He only just met this woman."

"Yes, but—"

"Marriage is a forever thing. A man needs to give it thought."

"And you assume he did not?"

"What I assume," he said, "is that I always thought a man should not leap into marriage as if he were leaping into the currents of a rampaging river."

She could feel the anger forming inside her. Or maybe it had been there all along, just waiting to surface.

"Your brother is not the only one who is leaping. The same applies to the woman."

Dante snorted with derision. "It isn't the same."

"Isn't it?" Her voice had gone from cool to frigid.

"Men are meant to be hunters. To roam. Women are meant to be gatherers. Of course it isn't the same."

Gabriella was looking at him as if he'd turned into an alien life form. Well, hell, he couldn't blame her. He knew he sounded like an idiot, but how could he not after finding Rafe's *Hey, man, I'm getting married!* e-mail in his inbox this morning? It had shaken him to the core.

Rafe, married?

It had to be a joke.

He'd phoned Rafe, got no answer, phoned Falco, got nothing there, connected with Nick who said, yeah, it was a shocker and, yeah, it was fast, and then he finally got through to Rafe who babbled like an idiot about how he'd fallen crazy in love even if he'd only married Chiara Cordiano the first time around so he could Do The Right Thing and then found he'd fallen head over heels in love.

"But marriage? So fast?" Dante had said.

And Rafe had said, yeah, why wait when you knew you'd found the right woman? A woman who loved you for what you were inside, not for what the world saw. Who loved you, just you, and could see herself growing old with you beside her. Who loved you for giving her your heart, not the things money could provide.

And in the blink of an eye, Dante had known Rafe could just as easily have been talking about him and his Gabriella.

About this "situation" that wasn't a "situation" at all but part of being deeply, totally in love.

He'd spent the day coming to grips with it, asking himself if Gabriella felt the same way, telling himself that she did, she had to, that she was not a woman who'd live with a man, sleep in his arms every night unless she loved him.

And, God, the whole thing was terrifying.

To declare his love for her, to offer his heart to her and hope she wouldn't reject it...

He'd thought about it, tried to figure out the best way to do it, delaying the moment because what would he do if she didn't feel the same and then, standing in the shower after putting Daniel to bed, the water sluicing down, he'd finally decided, okay, this was it, he'd just go out there and tell her he loved her, loved his son, that he couldn't live without them both...

"Dante," Gabriella said, and he swung toward her and caught her hands in his.

"Gaby." He spoke fast, afraid he'd lose his courage, wondering why it had taken him so long to come to his senses. "Gaby. Honey." He took a deep breath. "This thing tomorrow. My brother's wedding..." He swallowed hard; how come his mouth had gone so dry? "Taking you to it would be rough. You'd get dumped into the middle of my family and, trust me, we're not something out of a Hallmark card. My mother and my sisters would ask a million questions. My brothers wouldn't just ask questions, they'd do the Orsini version of the third degree. And my old man— Hell, where my father goes, so go the Feds. Plus, not a one of my family knows anything about this. You. Me. The baby." He paused only long enough to swallow again to moisten his throat. "So, here's the thing, Gabriella. I don't think—"

"I do not think so, either," Gabriella said. "The truth is, I would much prefer to avoid what promises to be an overly sentimental family reunion."

"What? No. See, you don't understand—"

"But I do. I understand perfectly." She drew her hands from his, gave him the kind of smile that made him understand the true meaning of a tight smile. "You say this wedding is tomorrow?"

"Right. Late morning. It'll all be over by noon."

"Excellent."

"Yes. I thought so, too. Because—"

"My attorney's name is Peter Reilly."

Dante blinked. "Huh?"

"His office is on Seventy-second Street. He handled any modeling contracts that were outside the purview of my agency."

"Gaby. What are you talking about?"

"I have been thinking, Dante. About our…our situation." *Do not cry,* she told herself fiercely. *Just because he's confirmed all your worst fears, just because he'd sooner do anything than introduce you to his family, you are not to cry!*

"Yes," he said slowly, "so have I. That's the reason I just explained things—"

"And a fine job of it you did," she said, and told herself how well she was doing. "I shall ask Peter a special favor, that he meet with us at his office tomorrow, even though it is a Sunday at, let us say, two in the afternoon."

"For what?" Dante said, totally bewildered.

This cold little speech, the frigid glare, that was what a man got for telling a woman that as rough as it was going to be, he wanted to take her to his brother's wedding? Tell his entire family he loved her? Tell them that she'd borne his child, that there would be another wedding as soon as they could get to the clerk's office Monday morning?

"For what?" he repeated, his eyes searching her face.

"For drawing up a payment schedule for what I owe you."

"What the hell are you talking about?"

"About resuming my own life," Gabriella said. "You see, I have been thinking things over. And it is time that happened. This has been very nice but—"

"Very nice?"

"You have been most kind to me. Of course, it would have been better had your attempt to buy the *fazenda* gone through."

"Better," he repeated, his voice low and dangerous. "Buying you the *fazenda* would have been better than bringing you to live with me?"

"Well, yes. It would have taken me a very long time to repay you but the *fazenda* was my home—"

"And this is not."

There was a terrible coldness in his voice. She wanted to put her arms around him, tell him that she had never been happier than she'd been the past days, that she wished, with all her heart, his home could really be her home, too…

"No," she said, struggling to hold on to what little pride she had left, "it is not."

They stared at each other while the silence of the chill night built around them.

Then Dante nodded.

"I'll want my attorney at this meeting."

"Certainly. I will give you my lawyer's address and telephone number."

"Do that."

He turned on his heel. Walked inside, grabbed his jacket, took the private elevator to the lobby and walked briskly into the night. When he got back, hours and hours later, his bed was empty.

Gabriella was in the guest suite.

Exactly where she should be, he thought grimly, and poured himself the first of the several brandies he figured he'd need before he could tumble into merciful sleep.

CHAPTER THIRTEEN

SUNDAY dawned bright and sunny.

A perfect day for a wedding, someone would probably say, but Dante knew better. It was a perfect day for a man to wake from a dream and realize he'd come within a heartbeat of putting his head in a noose.

He loved his brother, but better Rafe than him.

Dante showered, shaved, dressed and got out the door without seeing Gabriella. His mood was grim, but he wasn't sure why it should be, considering he'd barely escaped making the biggest mistake of his life. There was such a thing as carrying Doing The Right Thing too far.

He certainly hadn't been on the verge of asking her to marry him because he loved her.

Love?

Dante shuddered as he stepped from a taxi outside the unassuming little church in the Village where Rafe's wedding was to take place. Yesterday he'd done a good job of half convincing himself what he felt was love, but the truth was, love had nothing to do with it. Responsibility. That's what he felt for her. He was a decent man, she'd given birth to his child.

That was all there was to it.

Dante looked around as he straightened his tie. No cops.

No Feds. None he could spot, anyway. Rafe would, at least, be free of the kind of attention Cesare almost always received. This was Rafe's day, for better or for worse—no pun intended. He'd smile, toast his brother and his bride, then head for his meeting with Gabriella, her attorney and Sam Cohen. He'd phoned Sam at 6:00 a.m., and though Sam had grumbled, he'd said yeah, okay, he'd draw up the necessary documents—child support, child visitation—and hustle over to the two-o'clock meeting.

So, everything was a go. Have a meeting, move on with life. Today's agenda, in a nutshell.

Dante took a steadying breath, plastered what he hoped was a smile to his face and went up the stone steps into the old church.

At first he saw no one. Maybe, just maybe, Rafe had come to his senses…. Forget that. He could hear voices. His mother's, high and excited. His sisters, laughing and chattering like magpies. His brothers' low rumble. Another deep breath, and Dante headed for the small changing room where his family was gathered.

"Dante, *mio figlio,*" his mother shrieked, and embraced him in a hug that almost killed him.

"You finally got here," Anna said, but she tugged at his tie and kissed his cheek.

"We'd almost given up hope," Isabella added, but she smiled and kissed him, too.

His father gave him an inquisitive look.

"Dante."

"Father."

"Was your trip successful?"

Dante's mouth thinned. "This isn't the time to discuss it," he said coldly, and turned to Falco and Nicolo, who grinned.

"Hey, man," Falco said.

"Glad to see you made it," Nick said. "Where the hell have you been, anyway?"

"Away," Dante said.

Nick raised an eyebrow, but Rafe saved the day, grabbing him and saying, "Can you believe I'm doing this?"

Even Dante could tell the question was rhetorical. Rafe was smiling, and when he slid his arm around the waist of a beautiful, dark-haired stranger and drew her forward, the look he gave her was so filled with happiness that it put an ache in Dante's heart.

Had his eyes glowed that way each time he'd looked at Gabriella the past week? Hers had glowed when she'd turned them on him, but it had been a lie. All she'd ever wanted was that damned ranch...

"This is Chiara."

His new sister-in-law smiled shyly.

"Dante," she said softly, "I am very pleased to meet you."

She hesitated. Then she leaned in, stood on her toes and kissed his cheek.

Hell. She was starry-eyed with love, and that feeling came again, as if a hand had reached into his chest and grabbed hold of his heart. But then the organ began playing, Anna and Isabella rushed to Chiara's side and the next thing Dante knew, he was standing at the altar with his brothers.

The ceremony was brief. The women all cried. Rafe took his wife in his arms when the time came and kissed her with a tenderness that made Dante's throat tighten.

He swallowed hard. Gabriella had done one fine job, leaving him so confused that even he found today's events touching.

The reception was at their parents' home, in the big conservatory Cesare had built a couple of years ago.

Anna teased him about looking so grumpy.

"You could, at least, try looking happy," Izzy said. "This has been like a fairy tale!"

There were no fairy tales, Dante wanted to tell her, not in real life, but he smiled, said it sure was, picked up a flute of champagne and wandered over to Falco and Nick who were standing in a corner, looking out at their father's sea of withered tomato plants.

"Man," Nick said, sotto voce, "I think I'm on wedding-cake overload."

Falco agreed. "I'm glad Rafe's happy but if he tells me just once more how it's time I found myself a wife—"

Dante put the champagne flute on a table.

"How about we go someplace where nobody's gonna talk about the joys of matrimony?"

His brothers grinned.

Twenty minutes later, they were in their usual booth, the last one on the left, at The Bar.

The Bar wasn't fancy even though it was in a fancy location.

The reason was that the location had once been just a step up from a slum.

Back then, The Bar had been called O'Hearn's Tavern and was a neighborhood hangout downstairs from the hole-in-the-wall apartment Rafe had rented. But the brothers had liked the place. The beer was cold, the sandwiches and burgers were thick and cheap, and the no-nonsense ambience suited them just fine, though they'd probably have flattened anybody dumb enough to use the word *ambience* to describe the atmosphere.

Then, right about the time the four of them pooled their

resources and their skills to start Orsini Brothers, the area began to change. Tired old tenements, including the one where Rafe had lived, were gutted and reborn as pricey townhouses. An empty factory building became a high-priced club. *Bodegas* became boutiques.

Clearly, the Orsinis were about to lose their favorite watering hole.

So, they bought O'Hearn's. Stopped calling it that, started calling it, simply enough, The Bar. They had the leather booths and stools redone, the old wooden floor refinished and kept everything else unchanged: the long zinc bar, the battered wooden table tops, the thick sandwiches and burgers, the endless varieties of cold beer and ale.

Only the bartenders knew Rafe, Dante, Nick and Falco owned it. They wanted it that way. Their lives were high profile; The Bar was not…although, to their amazement, it became what was known as a "destination," which made the four of them laugh. It was where they often got together Friday nights and whenever they wanted to down a few beers, relax and talk.

Right now, though, nobody was relaxing. And that was Dante's fault.

The bar was shadowed, as always. Comfortable, as always. A Wynton Marsalis CD played softly in the background. The bartender, unasked, had brought Nick a bottle of Anchor Steam, Falco a Guinness, Dante a Belgian white. Their usual drinks, their usual booth, the usual cool jazz… but the atmosphere was tense.

Nick and Falco kept looking at each other, raising their eyebrows, rolling their eyes toward Dante.

What the hell's going on? they were saying in every way that didn't require speech, because neither of them wanted to ask. Dante's mood was, in a word, grim. His silence, his flat stare, the very set of his mouth made that painfully clear.

Still, even a brother's patience went just so far, and at last Falco decided to go for it.

"So," he said briskly, "you took the last couple of weeks off, huh?"

Dante looked up. "You got a problem with that?"

Falco's jaw shot forward. He started to answer but Nick silenced him by kicking him in the shin.

"Just asking," Nick said.

A muscle knotted in Dante's cheek. "I flew to Brazil last week. And took this week off. Okay?"

"What's doing in Brazil?"

The muscle in Dante's cheek took another jump. "I bought a ranch."

Falco and Nick looked at each other. "A ranch?"

Falco's question sounded more like "Are you nuts?" but Dante could hardly blame him. His brothers were trying to figure out what was going on. Well, hell, who could blame them? So he nodded, drank some beer, then looked across the table at the two of them.

"Correction. I almost bought a ranch. It was the old man's idea. I went down to buy it for him."

"Our old man was gonna buy a ranch?" Falco cackled. "That's a joke, right?"

"Actually," Dante said, after a beat of silence, "I ended up trying to buy it for myself."

"*You* were going to buy a ranch," Nick said, shooting Falco a worried look.

Dante drank some more beer. "Not for myself, exactly. For—for someone."

The brothers waited. Finally, Falco sighed. "Do we have to guess?"

"You remember a year ago? A little more than that. I was dating a woman."

"Wow," Nick said, "that's amazing. You, dating a—"

"Her name was Gabriella. Gabriella Reyes. A model."

Falco nodded. "Yeah. Tall. Hair a lot of different shades of gold. Spectacular legs. And what appeared to be one amazing pair of—"

"Watch your mouth," Dante growled.

His brothers raised their eyebrows.

"You want to tell us what's going on?" Nick said.

"No," Dante snarled...

And told them everything.

When he was done, nobody spoke.

He could see his brothers trying to take it all in. Hell, he'd have done the same in their place. A woman from the past. A baby. A ranch in foreclosure, a sneaky lawyer, an option that expired in twenty-four hours. It sounded like an old Western movie, except it was real.

Finally Falco cleared his throat.

"You're sure the kid is yours?"

"I'm sure."

"Because remember that time, years ago, Teresa Whatshername—"

"Gabriella is not Teresa Whatshername," Dante said sharply.

"No, no, of course she isn't. I only meant—"

"I know. Sorry. It's just— It's tough, you know?"

Nick leaned forward. "So, let me be sure I understand it all. You have a son."

"Cutest and smartest kid you ever saw," Dante said softly.

"But the woman who gave birth to him—"

"She has a name," Dante said, his voice sharp again. "Gabriella."

"Right. Gabriella. And she scammed you into buying this ranch—"

"Did I say that?"

"Well," Falco said, "you don't have to say it. From everything you told us, it's obvious."

"Nothing's obvious," Dante said coolly. "But, yeah, I bought the ranch for her." He gave a mirthless smile. "Thought I'd bought it, anyway."

"But you didn't."

"No."

"And the ranch is what she wanted."

Dante shrugged. "Yeah."

"So, no ranch. Instead, you brought her to New York. Moved her into your place. Accepted the kid as your own without asking for any proof—"

"The 'kid,'" Dante said, his tone plummeting from cool to icy, "is named Daniel. And I don't need proof. Gaby would never lie to me."

"Right," Nick said.

"She wouldn't. And I don't like the tone of your voice."

Nick nodded. Falco cleared his throat.

"And you took all these days off because…?"

A little lift of the shoulders. "It just seemed the right thing to do." Dante looked at Falco and Nick. Their expressions were benign, but something was lurking in their eyes, some truth they seemed to know and he didn't. "Gabriella was new to my place," he added. "New to the city."

"No, she isn't. She lived here. She worked here. You said so. She even knows your place, from when she dated you. So, try again, bro. You spent the time with her because…?"

Dante narrowed his eyes. "What's your point?"

Nick sighed. "I don't know, man. I mean, what could

my point possibly be? You were ready to drop five million bucks on a ranch for a woman. You acknowledged her baby as yours. You brought her home, moved her in, spent every minute with her and you tell us the relationship didn't mean a thing. Have I got the details right?"

Dante shrugged.

"You've got them right," Falco said. He looked at Dante. "Then, how come each time one of us so much as hints at her being anything but perfect, you turn purple?"

"I do not turn purple."

"He's purple now," Nick said lazily.

"He is, indeed," Falco agreed. "And we haven't even touched on why the lady's leaving you."

"No ranch. That's why."

"You don't think it could have anything to do with the fact that she suddenly realized she was living her life, living her kid's life, on your terms? That she has no money, no home, no anything here or back in Brazil that you don't graciously choose to dole out, and—"

Dante slammed down his beer bottle. "You make it sound as if I trashed her life. But that's not the way it was."

Falco narrowed his eyes. "How was it, then?" he said very quietly, and Dante's face all but crumpled.

"Oh, hell," he whispered. He looked up. "I loved her. I still do. I'm crazy for her. I want to marry her. Wake up every morning for the rest of my life with her beside me."

Nick arched an eyebrow. "But?"

"But last night, before I could tell her that, she turned cold as ice. Said it was time I met with her lawyer."

Falco nodded. "Seems to me it's one of two things happening here, bro. Either she's tired waiting for her ship to come in—"

Dante lunged for him. Falco grabbed his wrist.

"Take it easy, man, unless you think you and me taking

this outside will help calm you down." Dante didn't answer, and Falco let go of him and leaned over the table. "Or the lady loves you just the way you love her but she's got her pride, she's got the baby, and she's decided she'd rather end this on her terms than wait for you to do it."

"Why would she think that?"

"Maybe," Nick said patiently, "because you haven't said a word to her about what happens beyond today."

"Maybe," Falco added, "because of what you told us about how you broke up with her last time. The diamond earrings at dinner routine."

Dante was bewildered. "That's how we all do it."

Falco nodded. "Exactly."

"I don't know. I mean, I wanted to bring her to the wedding today. Introduce her to everybody." He gave a halfhearted laugh. "Of course, I warned her what it would be like, how rough it would be, what the old man is like, how Mama would probably go nuts learning she has a grandson, how the girls would swamp her, but before I could even finish talking, she interrupted, said she had no wish to go with me, that she wanted to discuss repaying the money she thinks she owes me…as if I'd take a dime from her."

"And how did she react to what you told her? That she'd be meeting us all at once?"

"I just told you," Dante said impatiently, "I never got that far. I just told her that— I told her that—" His face turned white. "*Merda!*"

"What?"

Dante shot to his feet. "I was preparing her for the big Orsini scene, but it must have sounded as if I were telling her there wasn't a way in hell I'd bring her with me today."

"The big Orsini scene?" Nick said, but Dante was already racing for the door.

Falco and Nick looked at each other. "He really loves her," Falco said.

"Sure seems like it."

"We could have left him in the dark."

"I know."

"But opening his eyes was the right thing to do."

"Still…"

"Still, another one bites the dust."

Nick shuddered and slipped from the booth.

"Man," Falco said, "don't tell me you're bailing, too?"

"I'm going to get us a bottle of Wild Turkey."

Falco nodded. "An excellent idea," he said, and decided they could wait until the bourbon was half-gone before they tried to figure out what in hell was happening to the Orsini brothers.

The beautiful morning had given way to a rainy afternoon.

New York plus rain. A simple equation that added up to no taxis in sight.

"Hell," Dante said, and started running.

A bus plowed by, the wheels spraying him with dirty water, and pulled in at a stop when he was halfway to his destination.

"Wait," he yelled, picked up his speed. He made it to the just-closing door, slipped and tore a very expensive hole in the very expensive left leg of his very expensive trousers.

Who gave a damn?

He got off the bus at Fifty-seventh Street, dashed into the store—open, thank God—and was outside again in less than ten minutes. A taxi was just pulling to the curb, a silver-haired gentleman was about to step into it. Dante tapped him on the shoulder.

"If I don't get this cab," he said, "I might just lose the woman I love."

The old guy looked him over, from his soggy Gucci loafers to his drenched Armani suit to his rain-flattened hair. Then he smiled.

"Good luck, son," he said.

Dante figured he was going to need it.

Gabriella's attorney's office was—it figured—on the top floor of a building that housed what seemed to be a non-working elevator.

He didn't give it a second try. Instead he took the old marble steps two at a time, stopped at the top only long enough to catch his breath and run his hand through his hair. Pointless, he thought, looking down at the puddle at his feet. Then he opened the office door and walked inside. The waiting room was empty, but straight ahead, through an open door, he could see a conference table. Gathered around it were Sam Cohen, a portly bald guy in tweed who had to be Gaby's lawyer.

And Gaby.

His Gabriella.

His heart did a stutter-step. *Here you go, Orsini,* he told himself. *This is your one shot at the rest of your life.*

"Gabriella."

They all turned and stared at him. He knew he had to look pretty bad. Sam Cohen's mouth dropped open. So did the other attorney's. Gabriella turned pale. She took a quick step toward him.

"Dante," she said, "*meu amor,* what happened to—" She stopped dead. Her chin rose. "Not that I care."

But she *did* care. The look on her face, the tremor in her voice, that wonderful word, *amor*… She cared. He just had to convince her that he cared, too.

"Gaby," he said, his eyes locked to hers, "sweetheart, please. Will you come with me?"

He held out his hand, held his breath…

She walked slowly to him. She didn't take his hand.

But he knew it was a start.

It was still raining.

Gabriella was wearing a raincoat, but the rain was already turning her gold-streaked hair wet and dark.

"Where are we going?" she demanded.

"Just into the park. See? The Seventy-second Street entrance is right across the way."

She looked at him as if he'd lost his mind. "On a day like this?"

"Gaby." Dante framed her face in his hands. "Please. Come with me."

She looked at him again. His hair was plastered to his head. His beautiful dark lashes were wet. Water dripped off his Roman nose. His suit would never be the same again and his shoes…

Her heart, which had felt as heavy as a stone since last night, seemed to lift just a little in her chest.

"Gaby," he said again, and then he lowered his head to hers and kissed her, lightly, tenderly, and even as she told herself his kisses meant nothing to her, she gave a little moan at the softness of his kiss. "Sweetheart. Come with me, I beg you."

So she did.

She kicked off her shoes, because how could you run in the rain wearing four-inch heels? And this time, when he reached for her hand, she let him take it.

He led her into the park, empty of everyone but a couple of glum-looking dog walkers. The rain was coming down harder; they ran faster and now she could see they were heading for The Boathouse restaurant. Was it open? It was.

At least the lounge was, but Dante drew her straight out onto the wet, deserted terrace.

"Sir," a voice said.

Dante ignored it.

"Sir," the voice said again.

Dante turned around, said a few words she could not hear to a waiter who looked at him as if he'd gone insane, but then the man laughed, said sure, if that was what he was determined to do...

And then they were alone.

Just she and Dante, and the rain.

Just she and the man she loved, would always love, in this place where she had foolishly opened her life to him, where she had foolishly admitted, if only to herself, that she loved him.

Why had she come with him? Why had she done again that which she had vowed she would not do, let Dante sweet-talk her into something that would seem wonderful for the moment and, ultimately, leave her weeping?

"Gabriella," he said, reaching into his pocket, taking out a small blue box...

She staggered back.

"No!"

"Gaby. Sweetest Gaby..."

"What is it this time?" she said in a horrified whisper. "A diamond pin? I do not want it!"

"It isn't a pin. It isn't a goodbye gift, baby. Take it. See for yourself."

"A gift to buy me back, then? Do you truly think I would permit you to do that? That I would let you—let you buy me, as you have tried to do these past two weeks..."

"Honestly, Gabriella..."

"Honesty be damned!" She was weeping now; salty tears running down her face and mingling with the sweet rain. "You are the least honest man I know, Dante Orsini! You made me think—you made me think that someday, someday you might…you might—"

"I love you."

"You see? There you are, lying again. If you loved me— oh, *Deus,* if you only loved me…"

She began to sob. Dante caught her in his arms, whispered her name, kissed her again and again until, at last, she kissed him back.

"I hate you," she whispered.

He smiled. "Yes. I can tell."

"Honestly, Dante—"

"Honestly, Gabriella." He drew back, just enough so he could lift the tiny package between them. "This is for you, sweetheart. Only for you, forever." He kissed her again. "Please," he said softly. "Open your gift."

She opened the little blue box only to silence him, to give herself time to get her emotions under control, telling him all the while that he had wasted his money, that she did not want whatever was in that box…

What was in that box was a diamond solitaire ring.

Gabriella stared at it. Then she stared at her lover. His smile was almost as bright as the diamond.

"I love you," he said. "I adore you. I always have. I was just too much a coward to admit it." It was wet on the terrace but what did that matter? Dante went down on one knee. "Marry me, Gaby," he said softly. "And let me make you happy forever."

She laughed. She wept. And when he rose to his feet to take her in his arms and kiss her, she flung her arms around his neck and kissed him back with all the love in her heart.

EPILOGUE

THEY were married in the same little church in Greenwich Village where Raffaele and Chiara had taken their vows.

Gabriella wore her mother's wedding gown. She had discovered it tucked away in the attic of the house in which she had grown up the weekend she and Dante flew to Brazil so he could finalize the purchase of the *fazenda*, which Andre Ferrantes had finally agreed to sell to him.

Gabriella said she had all a woman could ever want, she didn't need the *fazenda* to be happy, but Dante insisted Viera y Filho had to be hers. Hers, and their son's.

So, as Dante told his brothers, he'd made Ferrantes an offer he couldn't refuse. His brothers had laughed, though in truth, the offer had simply been for two hundred thousand dollars more than Ferrantes had paid for it. The man was a bully and a brute, but he wasn't a fool.

And so, Gabriella wore her mother's wedding gown. Her new mother-in-law's veil. "A tradition, *si?*" her new sister-in-law said.

"A tradition, *sim,*" Gabriella agreed, and the women smiled as they embraced.

Raffaele, Nicolo and Falco were Dante's best men. Anna, Isabella and Chiara were Gabriella's maids of honor.

Daniel, adorable and smiling, observed the ceremony from the protective arms of his happy, weeping grandmother.

Cesare stood silent, an enigmatic smile on his face, saying nothing to anyone until late in the day, when the reception in the Orsini conservatory was coming to an end.

"Nicolo," he said, walking up to his sons, "Falco, I would like to talk to the two of you."

"Father," Falco said, "it's been a long day."

"Right," Nick said. "It's getting late. We can talk another—"

"In my study."

Falco and Nicolo looked at each other. Nick shrugged.

"What the hell," he said.

Falco nodded. "Probably the same old same old about how he's getting on in years—"

"And the safe is there, the financial records are here—"

The brothers laughed and walked to the study door. Felipe, their father's *capo,* seemed to materialize from out of nowhere.

"You first," he said to Falco.

Falco and Nick rolled their eyes. Then Falco stepped into the room, Felipe closed the door and stood outside it, arms folded.

Nick sighed, and settled in to wait.

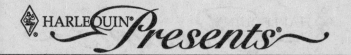

Bestselling Harlequin Presents author

Lynne Graham

brings you an exciting new miniseries:

PREGNANT BRIDES

Inexperienced and expecting, they're forced to marry

Collect them all:

DESERT PRINCE, BRIDE OF INNOCENCE
January 2010

RUTHLESS MAGNATE, CONVENIENT WIFE
February 2010

GREEK TYCOON, INEXPERIENCED MISTRESS
March 2010

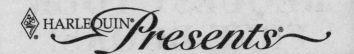

HARLEQUIN *Presents*

AT HIS
Service

From glass slippers to silk sheets

Once upon a time there was a humble housekeeper.
Proud but poor, she went to work for a charming and
ruthless rich man!

She thought her place was below stairs—
but her gorgeous boss had other ideas.

Her place was in the bedroom, between his
luxurious silk sheets.

Stripped of her threadbare uniform, buxom and blushing
in his bed, she'll discover that a woman's work has never
been so much fun!

Look out for:

POWERFUL ITALIAN, PENNILESS HOUSEKEEPER

by India Grey
#2886

Available January 2010

www.eHarlequin.com

REQUEST YOUR FREE BOOKS!

 HARLEQUIN® *Presents* ®

2 FREE NOVELS PLUS 2
FREE GIFTS!

PASSION GUARANTEED SEDUCTION

YES! Please send me 2 FREE Harlequin Presents® novels and my 2 FREE gifts (gifts are worth about $10). After receiving them, if I don't wish to receive any more books, I can return the shipping statement marked "cancel". If I don't cancel, I will receive 6 brand-new novels every month and be billed just $4.05 per book in the U.S. or $4.74 per book in Canada. That's a savings of close to 15% off the cover price! It's quite a bargain! Shipping and handling is just 50¢ per book*. I understand that accepting the 2 free books and gifts places me under no obligation to buy anything. I can always return a shipment and cancel at any time. Even if I never buy another book, the two free books and gifts are mine to keep forever.   106 HDN EYRQ 306 HDN EYR2

Name	(PLEASE PRINT)	
Address		Apt. #
City	State/Prov.	Zip/Postal Code

Signature (if under 18, a parent or guardian must sign)

Mail to the **Harlequin Reader Service:**
IN U.S.A.: P.O. Box 1867, Buffalo, NY 14240-1867
IN CANADA: P.O. Box 609, Fort Erie, Ontario L2A 5X3

Not valid to current subscribers of Harlequin Presents books.

Are you a current subscriber of Harlequin Presents books and want to receive the larger-print edition? Call 1-800-873-8635 today!

* Terms and prices subject to change without notice. Prices do not include applicable taxes. Sales tax applicable in N.Y. Canadian residents will be charged applicable provincial taxes and GST. Offer not valid in Quebec. This offer is limited to one order per household. All orders subject to approval. Credit or debit balances in a customer's account(s) may be offset by any other outstanding balance owed by or to the customer. Please allow 4 to 6 weeks for delivery. Offer available while quantities last.

Your Privacy: Harlequin Books is committed to protecting your privacy. Our Privacy Policy is available online at www.eHarlequin.com or upon request from the Reader Service. From time to time we make our lists of customers available to reputable third parties who may have a product or service of interest to you. If you would prefer we not share your name and address, please check here. ☐

HP09R

HARLEQUIN *Presents*

EXTRA

Presents Extra brings you
two new exciting collections!

MISTRESS BRIDES

*When temporary arrangements
become permanent!*

The Millionaire's Rebellious Mistress #85
by CATHERINE GEORGE

One Night In His Bed #86
by CHRISTINA HOLLIS

MEDITERRANEAN TYCOONS

At the ruthless tycoon's mercy

Kyriakis's Innocent Mistress #87
by DIANA HAMILTON

The Mediterranean's Wife by Contract #88
by KATHRYN ROSS

Available January 2010

I ♥ HARLEQUIN® *Presents*

BROUGHT TO YOU BY FANS OF
HARLEQUIN PRESENTS.

We are its editors and authors
and biggest fans—and we'd
love to hear from YOU!

Subscribe today to our online blog at
www.iheartpresents.com